THE
MINSTREL'S
TALE

THE
MINSTREL'S TALE

BERIT HAAHR

DELACORTE PRESS

Published by
Delacorte Press
an imprint of
Random House Children's Books
a division of Random House, Inc.
1540 Broadway
New York, New York 10036

Visit us on the Web! www.randomhouse.com/teens
Educators and librarians, for a variety of teaching tools, visit us at
www.randomhouse.com/teachers

Library of Congress Cataloging-in-Publication Data

Haahr, Berit I.
The minstrel's tale / by Berit Haahr.
p. cm.
Summary: When betrothed to a repulsive old man, thirteen-year-old Judith runs away, assumes the identity of a young boy, and hopes to join the King's Minstrels in fourteenth-century England.
ISBN 0-385-32713-7
[1. Runaways—Fiction. 2. Mistaken identity—Fiction. 3. Minstrels—Fiction. 4. Middle Ages—Fiction. 5. England—Fiction.] I. Title.
PZ7.H1113Mi   2000
[Fic]—dc21   99-049391

The text of this book is set in 13.5-point Granjon.
Book design by Susan Dominguez
Manufactured in the United States of America
August 2000
10 9 8 7 6 5 4 3 2 1
BVG

For Rachel and Elaine

PROLOGUE

Sir William listened, first unbelieving, then with increasing delight. *Finally,* he thought, *an apprentice worth training.* The boy was young, but it was clear that he had talent. Why, as far as William was concerned, the lad could begin his lessons that day. As William was music master at Eltham Palace, one of the King's country residences, his word, though not law, was generally honored.

The lad plucked the final notes on the harp and came to rest, looking up expectantly. *Young,* William thought again, *but with intelligent eyes. And he knows how to sit still*—which was more than one could say about most of the other boys William was training— boys of noble birth who had no interest in or constitution for the battlefield or the Church.

"Now sing," William commanded, handing the lad an eight-string lute. The boy paused to strum a few chords, making sure the instrument was properly tuned, then launched into a popular ballad.

"King Arthur lives in merry Carleile,
And seemely is to see,
And there he hath with him Queene Guenevere,
That bride soe bright of blee.

And there he hath with him Queene Guenevere,
That bride soe bright in bower,
And all his barons about him stoode,
That were both staunch and stowre."

William noticed the boy's quick fingering of the more difficult chords and cut him off after he had finished the second verse. "Well done, lad," he said, nodding approvingly. The boy had a clear voice; not a treble, unfortunately, but a strong, intense alto. *He'll probably be a baritone when it changes.* They always needed good boy sopranos, but a lad with such skill for playing the strings and pipes wouldn't be turned away because his voice was a little low. "Now, tell me your name."

"Jude, sir. Jude of Winchcombe." The boy relaxed visibly, and William suppressed a smile. The youth had almost been turned away from the castle when he

2

first appeared. No one could blame the guard. It seemed unlikely that such a scrawny and bedraggled waif could have any talent at all, let alone be such an accomplished musician that he'd be asked to stay. Even the fact that the lad traveled with a handsome peregrine falcon, a bird usually reserved for nobility, had done nothing to change the guard's opinion. But the boy had pulled a set of pipes from his pack and begun to play with startling skill. Only then had he been invited in, told to take off his traveling cloak and rest for a while.

Sir William had given the boy some coarse bread with hard cheese and a cup of strong ale, for the lad looked as if he hadn't eaten in days. He ate like it, too, wolfing down the bread and guzzling the ale, pausing only to wipe his mouth with the sleeve of his tunic. He then looked up and met William's gaze straight on, no wavering, with those light, intelligent eyes. For all his filthy clothing and coarse ways, the lad had obviously been taught some manners at one time—far back, by the looks of it. But the bones in his face and hands were fine, and he played the harp like the archangel Gabriel himself.

"Jude, eh? From Winchcombe?" The lad nodded. "And have you come all the way from there by yourself?" The boy hesitated, so William continued, "Come, lad, I won't scold you or send you away. It's clear that you've come alone."

"I can stay?" the boy asked eagerly, clutching the lute. William carefully removed the instrument from his hands—couldn't let him crush the delicate wood in his excitement. Jude let it go reluctantly.

William patted his shoulder. "Yes, lad, I think you belong with us. Just tell me how you got all the way to Kent on your own. And why."

"I came to be one of the King's Minstrels. I *had* to, ever since I heard one of your minstrels tell of the learned musicians here who train youngsters in music. I've wished to be a musician as long as I can remember." Jude took a deep breath and continued, looking into William's eyes all the time. "I was the youngest son, you see," Jude lied easily and without guilt. "My eldest brother, Stephen, will inherit the land, and Edmund became a priest, and Geoffrey and Henry are squires. I felt my father had done his duty to the Church and the King's forces already, and he could afford to send me here, to complete my training. But he had no time for music and little interest in storytelling. He said that I would bring him disgrace if I became a minstrel, and he forbade me. I was to be sent off, to become a page to Lord John, Earl of Bridgenorth. Instead, on the eve of my departure, I ran away. And thus I came here, to study with you."

"Well spoken." Sir William looked admiringly at the boy. Traveling more than fifty miles on his own— that took both courage and determination. The Master could only hope that Jude showed the same fortitude for lessons and music making. "Tell me, how many years have you?"

"Eleven," Jude lied again, steadfastly meeting William's eyes.

Shaking his head, Sir William exclaimed, "A mere babe! I'm certain the others will be delighted with your many tales." He clapped the boy on the shoulder and stood up. "Come, lad, let's get you some decent clothes and something more to eat. When was your last full meal?"

"I don't remember," Jude replied, glad of a question to answer truthfully. Hardly able to believe this good fortune, Jude followed Sir William from the small chamber into a stone passageway leading into the heart of the palace. Having traveled from Nesscliff, near Shropshire—easily a hundred and fifty miles farther away than Winchcombe—living off the land these past days, half starving, surviving on a combination of wits and hope: all this seemed less miraculous than the fact that Sir William believed the story Jude had told. That the Master hadn't discovered at the first moment they met that Jude was not Jude of Winchcombe, last-born son . . . but rather Judith of Nesscliff, youngest daughter of Lady Cecilia and stepdaughter of Lord Walter, Baron of Nesscliff. It had been her stepfather's idea that she be betrothed to the repulsive Lord Norbert. It had been Jude's idea to run away.

I

GWYNNA

*U*ntil her thirteenth year, Judith had been an obedient child. Of course, up until that time she had been raised in a convent school with daughters of other noblemen, where opportunities for disobedience were rare. The girls rose at dawn for prayers, breakfasted in silence, practiced sewing in the morning, assembled for more prayers and dinner, played music in the afternoon, prayed again, worked in the garden in clement weather, had more sewing or an occasional scholarly lesson in bad weather, ate supper, said their final prayers, and went to bed. Judith's only misbehavior had been during her first year at the convent. She was only seven or eight years old and, tired of the diet of dark, coarse bread and salt meat—or salt fish, on fast days—she had eaten some kind of cress from the garden. Judith remembered clearly sitting in that patch of the kitchen garden she was supposed to be weeding, and instead picking the greens and stuffing the leaves into her mouth. They'd been warm from the spring sun, and she'd chewed slowly, savoring the rich, bitter taste of the vegetable.

That was how she had been sitting when Sister Agatha found her. The nun had given the child a clout on the head and sent her to her cot for the rest of the day. Those greens had to feed the whole community, nuns, novices, and children; they weren't for the sole enjoyment of any one person. Judith had no supper that night, nor breakfast nor dinner the following day. When she was finally allowed supper that second day, she ate her coarse bread and salt pork gratefully. She was a model pupil from that day on.

It wasn't difficult for Judith, once she had adjusted to the meager diet. Most of the sisters were kind and rarely beat the girls. Judith stayed out of Sister Agatha's way. She applied herself to learning all manner of fine and everyday needlework, hemming napkins and embroidering handkerchiefs with skill, if not enthusiasm. The nuns taught her about Heaven above and Hell burning hotly within the round, still Earth; they told her of the nine choirs of angels in Heaven, and the seven planets beneath it. She learned her prayers in Latin, spoke English and French, wrote and read quite well for a girl, and could even do some simple arithmetic. But in her music lessons Judith came to life.

When the harp or lyre or flute was brought out, Judith did all she could to hold back, but her love of music and her natural ability made it almost impossible not to surpass the others. Not everyone approved. Sister Brigid, who gave the music instruction, had pulled Judith aside early on to explain.

"You're here to learn to play and sing adequately, Lady Judith. Your future husband will want you to entertain him and his guests on quiet nights. But there will be many others who will play and sing at his bidding—true musicians and minstrels. He wouldn't like for his wife to be making a minstrel of herself, or to be thinking that she was special or closer to God because of her talents. We are sinners all. You may play the harp with talent, child, but that makes you no closer to the angels than the rest of us."

"But, Sister," Judith ventured—not knowing yet that questioning one of the sisters was considered presumptuous—"my father told me that music was for the glory of God."

Sister Brigid sighed and clasped her rosary, as if Judith were trying her infinite patience. "And who was your father, to understand the ways of our Creator? Go, child, it's time for Vespers; go and contemplate your wickedness. Beseech our Lord for his forgiveness, for those who sin without repentance most surely face the fiery pits of Hell."

Judith, her face scarlet with shame, crept out of the chamber. Neither her mother nor her father had ever called her wicked, nor threatened her with damnation when she misbehaved. Tears filled her eyes, for her father was dead and could never again comfort her. Afraid that Sister Brigid would catch her crying and scold her for further wickedness, Judith rubbed her sleeve vigorously across her eyes and nose before joining the others in chapel.

Because unnecessary speech was frowned upon, and because the girls were almost never left unsupervised, friendships among the pupils were rare and superficial. As one of the youngest girls, Judith typically spoke little to the others, but she would generally join in the illicit, whispered conversations about food. That night, however, she picked at her salt cod without comment and did not complain under her breath or say she wished she were at home eating roast pheasant, soft cheese, and fresh greens. Only Lady Gwynna, one of the younger girls with red hair and merry green eyes, seemed to know that something was wrong.

Gwynna had been sent away from home early because her mother, a beauty from Wales with flame-colored hair and a sharp tongue to match, had said that the child was the only one of the family with a brain in her head, and that the nuns would teach her more than Gwynna's addlebrained sisters and father. To be fair, Gwynna's father, an earl and a member of the King's London court, was less addlebrained than bullied by his hot-tempered wife. He adored her and wished to keep her happy, even while he prayed nightly that she would calm herself and not make a spectacle of the family at court. Gwynna and her sisters often wondered why the unlikely pair had married, but Sabrene, who was the eldest, said that grown people often did silly things for love and regretted them later on.

But Gwynna's story was happier than Judith's, as she discovered that night after evening prayers. Her cotmate sound asleep, Gwynna eased off her pallet and crept down the center of the long room. She appeared like an apparition before Judith, who lay crying silently into the straw-stuffed mattress. Suddenly seeing the figure in white standing above her, Judith sat bolt upright with a gasp. For a second she'd thought Gwynna the Angel of Death, come to take her away because of her sins.

Gwynna shushed her—not that anything could wake large, snoring Abigail, with whom Judith shared the narrow mattress on the floor. At the other girl's silent urging, Judith slid out carefully from the covers. Abigail immediately rolled over, taking up the whole of the pallet, flinging her arm over the side and mumbling in her sleep. Covering her mouth to smother her laughter, Gwynna took Judith's hand and pulled her over to the doorway.

In the next room the novices, as the newly joined nuns were called, all seemed to be asleep. The corridor was dark, save for a bit of moonlight shining through the window cut high in the stone wall. The two girls stood contemplating one another in the gloom.

"Why were you crying?" Gwynna finally asked, her voice so low it was hardly a breath in the still night air.

"I wasn't crying," Judith breathed back. She feared the other girl would report her to the nuns, for tears were thought to be self-indulgent.

"Yes, you were. And you hardly ate that poor slop they call supper. What's wrong?"

Even in the darkness, Judith could sense the other girl's concern, her friendliness. With the gratitude of someone who had longed for a confidante, Judith softly poured out her story. She paused only once, frozen at a chance noise from the novices' dormitory, then continued when all was silent again.

Her father, a knight with a minor holding in Nesscliff, had gone with his small army to battle for the King, as he did almost every spring. But last year, he had not returned, nor had Judith's eldest brother, Stephen. Her dear father, who had taught her to play the pipes and had called her "my merry little Jude," and who had always had time for her, even when he was

12

involved with manor business, had been killed in a skirmish with some rebellious Scotsmen. Judith ached for her father. She missed his cheerful presence in the manor and the winter evenings when he had leisure time to spend singing with his youngest daughter. While Judith had inherited her mother's fair coloring and fine bones, she took after her father in most other ways—her height, her intelligence, her love of music and stories.

Lady Cecilia was not much of a mother. Married at thirteen, she'd given birth to five babies in seven years, only one of which died in the first year. After Judith's birth—a difficult one, with labor lasting all one day and into the next—Cecilia took to her chamber, with her three gentlewomen, her unmarried older sister, and her little dog, and rarely came out again. She suffered from melancholia, the physician said, brought on by an overabundance of black bile. He prescribed juniper and wormwood tea and told her to lie with an agate stone next to her stomach. But despite the physician's frequent attendance and her ladies' constant care, Cecilia was ill most of Judith's early life and rarely strayed from her chamber or her favorite little garden, even on feast days.

In a household composed almost entirely of men, Judith's world was a small one, made up of a few women and an occasional male page sent to wait upon her mother. Her sister Elinor, older by only two years, was Judith's most regular companion, along with their nurse and their ladies' maid, Molly, the daughter of the bailiff. Cecilia could not spare one of her own gentlewomen to care for the children. A chamberer to attend the gentlewomen and a laundress were the last members of this female enclave that existed within the larger male household, inhabiting small chambers rather than the great hall and rarely mixing with the men.

Molly was not much older than the girls themselves, but she helped them wash and dress in the morning, and oversaw their needlework, and kept them occupied so they wouldn't trouble their poor mother. It was Molly whom Cecilia sent to tell the girls that their father and eldest brother were dead; later it was Molly, too, who told them that Judith was being sent to the Convent of the Devout Sisters of the Holy Lamb, and that Elinor, at age nine, was now betrothed to young John, Baron of Lichfield, and would be going to live with his family until the wedding.

But that was only after Judith and Elinor found out by chance that their own mother was to wed again, even though their father was barely cold in his grave. They had sought her out one night, when the snow was packed high against the manor walls, when even huddling with Molly under the many covers couldn't warm their frozen feet. They wanted their mother. They knocked on her chamber door, waiting impatiently in the drafty passageway for Cecilia to call for them to enter, or for one of her gentlewomen to open the door. This night, however, they were greeted by their uncle Walter, their father's eldest brother.

Elinor, being older and wiser, grasped the situation immediately and grabbed Judith's hand to back away. Judith, not understanding, spoke. "We want to see our mother, to warm us up."

Walter cupped the girl's face in his large, hairy hand, looking down at her with a smile on his lips, but with cold eyes. "Warm yourself tonight, child. Begone." He gave her a push away from the chamber and shut the door behind him. The very next morning, Lord Walter announced his betrothal to Lady Cecilia. Cecilia's unmarried sister, Catherine, had been conspicuously absent from morning Mass; she was packing to make the journey back to Maesbrook, where another sister lived.

"Had Lady Catherine wanted to marry your uncle Walter?" Gwynna whispered to Judith. Gwynna sensed, rather than saw, Judith nod. "And your sister was sent off to live with this baron from Lichfield?" Again Judith nodded. "No wonder you're crying!"

This remark set off a fresh burst of tears. Gwynna hushed Judith, then pulled her close and let her cry. Before long, the shoulder of Gwynna's heavy nightdress was thoroughly soaked. At last Judith pulled away, sniffed softly, and quieted herself.

"I'm sorry to make such a spectacle of myself, Lady Gwynna," she said formally.

"For the reverence of God!" Gwynna said with great feeling. "You're allowed to cry. Whatever happened today to remind you of your melancholy?"

Judith told her about the scene with Sister Brigid. Gwynna shook her head slowly. "You've never before been called wicked? Why, my mother calls the whole lot of us wicked at least five times a day, and that's before we even reach morning Mass. This uncle Walter of yours—he sent you away, but he never called you wicked?"

"Aye. Elinor and I tried not to cross his path. And it was only a matter of weeks before we were gone from the manor."

"Will you see your sister again?"

"For her wedding," Judith said with a sigh.

A looming gray figure appeared before them. The girls started and clutched each other, only to be reprimanded by one of the novices, awakened by their chatter, which had grown louder as the two girls talked.

"Please don't tell the sisters," Gwynna begged. "Lady Judith had a nightmare, and I was comforting her."

The novice, though grumpy at being wakened in the middle of the night, had pity. She sent the girls to bed again, promising not to tell. Gwynna gave Judith's hand a quick squeeze before heading to her own pallet.

Judith wriggled onto her mattress, feeling enormously better. She shoved Abigail over, made herself comfortable, and fell asleep.

Life was much more pleasant at the convent with a friend to confide in. Not that they had much time together. But a stray word, whispered between prayers and a meal, or even a friendly look across the chamber, was enough. Judith felt less alone in the world, knowing there was at least one person at the convent who understood her.

Judith traveled to Lichfield the next year to witness the nuptials of Elinor and Lord John. Elinor glowed with shy happiness at her young bridegroom; she seemed—it appeared to her grieving younger sister—delighted with the match, and with becoming a baroness before the age of eleven. Her future was secure. Following the wedding Judith spent a month in Nesscliff with her morose, ailing mother, and was relieved finally to return to the convent.

Gwynna made the longer trip to London for her sister's wedding. Sabrene had made an even better match than Elinor: her betrothed was an earl with both wealth and connections to the royal family. Their father was in extremely good humor and had made arrangements for Gwynna to marry the eldest son of another prosperous earl with ties to the King. Gwynna was initially distressed at the news—she was only nine, after all, young to be betrothed—but after she met her intended, Lionel, she changed her mind. He was tall, with curly brown hair and light eyes, and appeared altogether handsome and kind. And he was only seventeen.

Aside from the weddings, the two girls did not return home again until it was time to leave the convent. They had received periodic letters, of course, telling of important news—the birth of Judith's two stepbrothers, a year apart; her older brother Edmund's graduation from novice to priest; Gwynna's sister's babies, and so on. The news always seemed unreal, somehow, to girls whose days were so shaped by the cloister. Even major events of state they learned about only from the nuns. Thus the coronation of young King Edward III, his marriage the next year to Philippa of Hainaut, and the birth of their son, Edward the Prince of Wales, were not the marvelous celebratory events they would have been at home. There was little festivity in the convent, even on holy days.

Finally, at the ages of thirteen and fourteen, respectively, Judith and Gwynna were called before the prioress and told they were leaving to start their true lives. Gwynna was returning to London to become a countess; her betrothed was now an earl, since the death of his parents during a fire. Lionel wished to wait no longer for his nuptials, and Gwynna's mother had finally deemed the girl fit for noble company. Judith, however, had no idea what suitors would await her in Nesscliff, but her stepfather had written the prioress that Judith's sojourn at the cloister must come to an end. She could speak three languages, read and write a little in each, sew and embroider with great skill, and was a master musician, though no one had ever informed her of that fact. All her stepfather cared about was that she was now of an acceptable age for marriage, and there was no need for him to pay her upkeep when another man might take the burden off his hands.

Judith and Gwynna packed their meager belongings and bade good-bye to the sisters and the other girls. Gwynna's departure day came first, and when her father's steward arrived to retrieve her, she and Judith held on to one another mutely before saying farewell. The rest of their lives were planned out for them. And even though neither knew anything about running a household or raising children, both were going home to be married.

II

THE MINSTREL

"*L*ord Norbert, the Baron Caerleon, Lord of Chepstow and Usk, may I present to you Lady Judith of Nesscliff?" Lord Walter said with great solemnity. He placed Judith's slender hand in the large, spotted hand of an old, bearded man. At least he looked old to Judith. Lord Norbert bowed low, giving her hand a lingering kiss. Judith shuddered, and her stomach ached. Her stepfather had already finished negotiating her dowry when she had arrived back from the convent. This was the man she was going to marry.

Maybe he's only forty, Judith thought, trying to suppress the panic that was rising in her, as she was led to the table for the feast in honor of their betrothal, and of Norbert's acceptance of her.

"His poor wife died in childbed," Molly had informed Judith as she helped the girl dress in a light blue gown with delicate white lace at the neck, wrists, and hem, a great change from the simple gown she had worn at the convent. But Judith couldn't enjoy it, not the ornate gown, nor the darker blue mantle placed on her shoulders, nor the fine white netting with which Molly dressed her long golden hair.

"How many children did they have?" Judith whispered, dreading the answer.

"Lo, but five or six," Molly replied. "The last died with his mum, and it was the first boy-child aborn. His lordship seems much hurrying to find another wife, to birth him an heir."

As stepmother, thus, Judith would have in her charge "five or six" girls, three of whom she subsequently learned were older than she. For, Molly whispered the gossip to her, Norbert refused to let any of them marry, in case one produced a male heir. He'd have the girls die old maids before he would marry them off and have his property inherited by the son of some other man's loins. He was also unwilling to pay dowries for his daughters, being of a miserly nature and considering girls a waste of good gold and oxen.

Needless to say, Judith was terrified as she took her place beside him at the banquet. She tried to quiet her breathing as the chaplain said grace and a special memorial for the day's saint, Barnabas the Apostle. For the first time, Judith was eating in the great hall, seated on the dais with her stepfather and his noble guests. Gentlemen and yeomen occupied other long tables, and the noise in the hall seemed deafening. The ewerer poured water over Judith's hands from an enamel pitcher, and a yeoman placed before her a trencher of her own, on a silver platter—her own bread, for once. Her appetite of convent days, however, was gone: the delicacies that passed in front of her might as well have been dark bread and salt fish, for all she could eat. Dates stuffed with cheese, leeks with walnuts, and spiced chestnut cream all were offered to her by the attending yeomen. She picked at the venison with currant-wine sauce, the swan meat with parsley and pine nuts, the fish cakes.

Norbert, wishing to fatten up the young thing at the expense of her stepfather, piled dumplings, tarts, and sweetmeats onto her trencher. But Judith could hardly eat and couldn't bear to speak with the coarse man seated at her right. Nor did it do her any good that her stepfather was seated across from her. Walter stared at her as he ate, demanding silently, as he fed bits of meat off his knife to the falcon that perched on his forearm, that she be amiable to the man who was her betrothed. Judith would have found it difficult to eat under any circumstances with the beady eyes of both man and bird following her every move.

Even the fact that Elinor was seated near her at the

grand table could not cheer Judith, for Elinor was clearly with child again. She had made the journey from Lichfield to spend the month helping her sister prepare for the wedding. Seeing Elinor's bulging form simply served to remind Judith of her own fate. Only when the minstrel arrived did she revive a bit.

The young minstrel wore a hood with a tail that fell down his back and a cape with an ornamental edge. He carried a rebec, a lute, a tambourine, and a drum all strung from his body, and pipes in his belt pouch, but he placed the instruments on a stone bench while he drank some ale. Giving the tambourine a good smack to get everyone's attention, he picked up the lute and started strumming. In no time, the hall was filled with his sweet tenor, which was joined by the voices— some sweet, others not so—of the feasters. Judith sang out loud and clear, earning the minstrel's approving nod.

> *"Summer is a-coming in,*
> *Loude sing cuckoo!*
> *Groweth seed and bloweth meed,*
> *And springeth the wood now.*
> *Sing cuckoo!"*

After the well-known Cuckoo Song, the minstrel played "The Three Ravens," and a ballad about King Arthur and the marriage of his knight Sir Gawain, which Judith had never before heard. She picked up the tune quickly, but decided, if she had a chance, she'd ask the young minstrel to teach her the words. Afterward he sang some bittersweet songs: "Lullaby" and "The Two Sisters," the latter of which made Judith shed tears, because it reminded her of Gwynna, and that she herself would soon be off to Chepstow, wed to this man on her right. Lord Norbert hadn't even bothered to look up from his plate to watch the minstrel; he just gobbled food and guzzled wine throughout the entertainment.

The minstrel finished with "The Ballad of Thomas Rhymer," which made everyone laugh and cheer the young fellow. Then, slinging the small lute over his shoulder, he started making his rounds of the tables, ale cup in hand.

"And is your name Thomas, like in the song?" Judith's stepfather called. He was well into his cups at that point, pleased with the banquet and the prospect of marrying off his wife's last daughter.

"Nay, sir. 'Tis but Robin, like the infamous Robin Hood and his squires, of the ballads."

"And do you take from the rich and give to the poor, like Robin the bandit?" Lord Walter slurred.

"Nay, sir," Robin the minstrel repeated with a grin. "For I give to the rich"—here he held up his lute— "and demand only *this* in payment." He now held up his ale cup.

Lord Walter roared with laughter and threw the minstrel a shilling. Robin caught the coin deftly and slipped it into his belt pouch, then strummed a few chords on the lute. "And who is this sweet-voiced nightingale?" Robin asked, gesturing toward Judith.

Lord Walter boomed, " 'Tis my stepdaughter. This banquet is her betrothal feast."

Robin quickly took in the way Judith grimaced, the leer of the old man sitting next to her, and Lord Walter's acrimonious tone. *Poor girl,* he thought. *And with a voice like that. Such a waste.*

Aloud he addressed Judith. "My lady, on the occasion of your betrothal, I must honor you with a special song." He then spoke to Lord Walter. "Good sir, may your stepdaughter join me for more singing and playing?" He gestured toward a nearby bench, where his other musical instruments lay. Lord Walter waved a hand dismissing the two—he didn't care. Lord Norbert, however, followed the pair with angry eyes as Judith gratefully allowed herself to be led to the stone bench.

"Do you play as well as sing, m'lady?"

"Please call me Judith. Do not humble yourself before me." She added under her breath, "Someone as talented as you should not have to humble himself before anyone, especially not before louts such as my stepfather and husband-to-be." Making a face, she reached for the lute.

Robin smiled, picking up his drum. "Lady Judith, one learns as a traveling minstrel *always* to humble himself before the lord of the manor. One may ridicule him later in song and pantomime, but one is always courteous to his face."

Judith laughed, conscious of being lighthearted for the first time since she had parted from Gwynna at the convent. "Would you teach me that ballad about King Arthur and Sir Gawain? I much enjoyed it."

Before long, Judith was strumming the tune on the lute while Robin beat time on his drum.

> *"King Arthur welcomed them there all,*
> *And soe did Lady Guenevere his Queene,*
> *With all the nights of the Round Table,*
> *Most seemely to be seene.*

> *King Arthur beheld that lady faire,*
> *That was soe faire and bright,*
> *He thanked Christ in Trinity,*
> *For Sir Gawain that gentle knight."*

The two musicians harmonized softly together, their pure tenor and alto unnoticed by the increasingly drunken guests at the banquet. Other minstrels and musicians strolled around the tables, entertaining. Judith and Robin weren't missed, not even by Walter and Norbert, who were well into their second wine-skin by then.

Robin and Judith finished the ballad and launched into another. The evening passed quickly as they shared songs, teaching each other new tunes. Judith played the pipes while Robin sang, and later took a turn with the drum. " 'Tis a pity you're a lass," Robin said quietly when they'd put down their instruments for a rest. "You would find a warm welcome with the King's Minstrels."

Judith blushed and ducked her head. Not only was she an excellent singer and player, Robin thought, but she was quite pretty, too. A mite tall for a girl, and rather too thin, but her hair shone like gold in the candlelight of the great hall, and her eyes were a startling light blue.

"I've heard about the King's Minstrels," Judith whispered. "At His Majesty's palace?"

Robin nodded. "Aye, Eltham Palace, in Kent. 'Tis a musician's paradise. Not that we don't work hard, mind you, but to spend all day practicing and making tunes . . . 'twas a dream come true for me."

"Why do you travel, then?" Judith asked. She strummed a few experimental chords on the lute, testing the fingering on one of the songs Robin had just taught her.

" 'Tis part of the work, Lady Judith," he answered, smiling at her. "We must show the lords of the countryside that we haven't been sitting idle at Eltham." He lowered his voice to a whisper. "We also bring news to far-flung friends, and take news back to the King." Robin straightened up then and took another hasty swig of ale. He'd never told the King's business to strangers before. Strangely enough, this tall girl with the light eyes seemed to be bewitching him, making him forget his usual caution. He would find it difficult to leave the castle in the morning, knowing that this enchanting girl was to be wed to that foul old man.

Unaware of the indiscretion, Judith was charmed by the minstrel and his tales of Eltham Palace, and by the new tunes he brought. It amazed and honored her that this young musician, who might even have met the King himself, was willing to single her out. After so many years at the convent when she had been told that she wasn't special, that her music wasn't a particular talent, here was evidence to the contrary. She grew bold in her questioning.

"And how does one become a minstrel for the King?"

Robin was relieved that she hadn't probed further about the minstrels' other business. "Since we travel to castles and manors all over Britain, and perform at feasts and festivals, we have the chance to hear all sorts of lads sing and play and tell stories. We'll single out a boy who has a special talent and speak to his father. If he has plans for the boy—if the lad is the heir, or is already promised as a page—then we go our way. But, if the boy is a younger son and has no interest in the responsibilities of knighthood—which, I can tell you, my lady, often happens with musical boys—then we take him to train at the palace. The boys are delighted. No one has ever told them that they have any choice but to go to battle. We'll do the same for the son of a wealthy merchant or judge, trusting that the boy has the refinement for courtly society."

"Are there ever any girls?" Judith asked hopefully, knowing already the answer would be no. But wedding Lord Norbert was surely worse than going to battle.

Robin felt his heart melt. For a moment, he allowed pity to show in his eyes. At eighteen, Robin had traveled little, but he knew how often young girls were married off to rich older men, like so many lambs being taken to market. He struggled to find the right words, but even as he did so, he knew, looking into Judith's sad eyes, that she wasn't expecting any good news from him. "I'm sorry, my lady. I wish there were."

Lord Norbert chose this moment to burst in on their conversation. He had been watching his young betrothed and that cheeky minstrel fellow with increasing fury. It was *his* feast, celebrating *his* betrothal. He wasn't going to stand for this any longer, seeing another man—a sneaky rogue of a musician, at that—paying court to his lady. Norbert had risen shakily to his feet and stumbled over to the pair in the corner.

"Come, miss, 'tis time you returned to your husband-to-be." He clapped his hand on Judith's shoulder and turned her to face him. Judith pulled her head back at the foul scent of his breath.

"Aye, m'lord," she answered meekly. She shot Robin an apologetic look. The minstrel could barely control his rage at the disgusting drunken lord. He made a courtly bow to Judith. " 'Twas a pleasure tuning with you, m'lady."

"That's enough of your lip, knave," Norbert slurred. He began to pull Judith back to the dais, mentally vowing never to have any minstrels at his manor, if he ever had a feast. Which was unlikely since he would have to feed all those hungry mouths out of his own pocket.

Only Robin's knowledge that he was an emissary of the King enabled him to swallow the insult and turn back to his instruments. He seethed silently, watching Norbert lead Judith back to the table. Robin almost reached for his concealed belt knife when Norbert put his hand on the girl's backside as he settled her onto the long bench, but the minstrel again controlled himself. The girl was betrothed, after all. There was nothing he could do.

Judith felt Lord Norbert's hand on her bottom and

she stiffened and tried to pull away. He gave a drunken cackle and pinched her—hard—before removing his hand. Judith flushed a violent red and blinked away tears. In her thirteen years, no man had ever touched her in that way. It was a sin, she knew from the nuns. When she was married, however, she would have to allow Lord Norbert that and all sorts of other liberties. She swallowed hard, looking down the table at her pregnant sister. Judith was unsure whether she would be able to keep down the little food she had swallowed during the meal.

It was well past midnight when the guests began to retire. After an evening of being pawed and fondled by the drunken Lord Norbert, Judith simply wanted to throw herself into bed and howl about her upcoming nuptials. Elinor, however, was already sprawled across the mattress they shared, snoring gently. Her swollen body and the feather pillows she had heaped around herself left little room in the bed. Weeping silently, Judith managed to squeeze herself into a comfortable spot next to her sister and tried not to think about the future.

III

ELINOR

"*T*he minstrel left you a gift, Judith." Lord Walter spoke roughly the next morning as they broke their fast, dropping the set of pipes carelessly onto the table. Walter's head ached from last night's wine, and he wished all the guests in the manor would stop shouting so. He nursed his poor head, sipping a cup of ale. He had no appetite for food.

Judith took the small wooden instrument reverently, her fingers automatically touching the holes on the top. She started to play a scale, delighted at the clear tones, then took the pipes from her mouth abruptly when she saw how her stepfather winced. No need to make him angry, not on a morning like this. "He's gone, then?" she asked, laying the instrument across her lap.

"Aye, at first dawn." Walter took another sip of ale.

"He apologized that he wouldn't be at your wedding, but he had other business to attend to. He left that as your wedding gift."

"Was that all he said?"

"Nay, he made all manner of flowery speeches. You know what word-spinners those minstrels be." Walter grunted and held his pounding head. Judith knew she'd get no more out of him.

Still cradling the instrument in her hand, she returned to her chamber after her hurried meal. Before entering she peeked inside, to make certain that no guests were there, busy instead touring the grounds or keeping Lady Cecilia company. Relieved that the room was empty, Judith settled herself into a favorite cushioned wooden chair and was playing away when Elinor entered, a square of cloth in her hands. She smiled at Judith, and lowered her large form onto another chair to begin her embroidery. They sat companionably for many minutes, one sister tuning, the other sewing, and Judith realized how much she missed Elinor. And how much more she would miss her after she'd been wed and sent away to Chepstow.

She hit a sour note on the pipe and winced. Elinor looked up from her needle. "A lovely instrument. 'Twas generous of the minstrel to leave it for you. For your wedding." She looked at Judith with knowing eyes.

Judith ignored her meaning, working instead on the

fingering of the note she had just missed. Something sounded different than it had last night. The tone of the pipes was duller. Was it her playing? She held the instrument up to the light coming in from the window, peering into the small hollows.

"Is there something the matter?" Elinor asked with mild curiosity.

"It looks . . . it looks as if there's something caught inside!" Judith exclaimed, perplexed by the light form stuck inside the smallest reed. She poked her finger carefully into the reed, but whatever it was eluded her grasp. With a sigh, she looked around the room for something smaller to poke inside. Finally she seized an ornate brooch, and with the pin began to drag the offending item out of the instrument. After a minute a white corner showed, and she gingerly pulled it the rest of the way out.

It was a small piece of parchment, folded square and secured somehow inside the instrument's hollow. Elinor looked over with interest. Judith unfurled the square and studied the unfamiliar hand, in brown ink, on the sheet. In French was written: *Should you meet a boy with musical talent, send him to me at the palace. He shall be well taken care of there.* Below was a scrawled *R,* next to the drawn outline of a lute—the symbol for minstrels and musicians. On the back, a brief sketch of a map showed the way from Lord Walter's manor in Nesscliff to Eltham Palace in Kent.

Judith caught her breath, staring at the parchment. Unable to control her trembling, she handed the sheet to her sister, who was craning her neck to see. Elinor studied the map with interest, then asked Judith to tell her the words. At home, Elinor had been taught to read the alphabet and some Latin prayers, but, since she had never been to school, that was all she could read.

Judith read to her. Elinor's eyes flicked from the page of words to Judith's face. "Are you sure that's all it says? It's not a love note, is it?"

Judith blushed but met her sister's gaze. "No, it is not. 'Tis something better. The minstrel is telling me to go to the palace, to become one of the King's Minstrels."

Elinor dropped the embroidery into her lap and laughed, startled by Judith's words. "What kind of addlebrained idea is that? If you're telling the truth, the note says 'a boy with musical talent,' not a girl who's about to be wed. Are you sure the letter doesn't ask you to run away with him?" she asked suspiciously.

"When have I told you untruths?" Judith demanded, exasperated that her sister didn't understand. Elinor was married to a kind and handsome lord, not a drunken ogre. Judith shuddered inside, remembering Lord Norbert's hands on her at last night's banquet. She could not marry him. She would not.

Elinor sighed. "I do not know, Judith. I do not understand you now. You're set to wed Lord Norbert within the month; what is this talk of becoming a musician? You're a *girl,* Judith, not a boy with talent. Why do you think this message is for you?"

"It's written this way so if our stepfather discovered the missive, he would not go after Robin the minstrel and kill him, which he would do if the note said 'Come, Judith, run away instead of marrying that old goat.' "

"Judith! You shouldn't speak that way about your betrothed!" Elinor scolded halfheartedly. She was nodding also, knowing Judith was right about one thing: their stepfather would kill any man who dared suggest such a thing. He might kill Judith, too, if she were so disobedient. Elinor grabbed her sister's arm. "You can't run away. His lordship would be mightily displeased. He would punish you most severely."

"Only if he found me. And I have no intention of being found." Judith stood and paced around the chamber. "Robin wasn't asking me to run away; he was just letting me know that there is a safe place for me to run to. Last night, he saw the same thing I did: I cannot marry that pig. I would kill myself first."

Utterly shocked, Elinor stood and grabbed her sister's hand. Running away was a sin, but suicide . . . even talk of suicide was a sin against nature. "Lord Walter will kill you," she whispered. "Or you'll be attacked on the road by thieves and murderers. How can you travel alone?" A sob caught in her throat. She sat back down, clutching her bulging stomach with her arms. She might see her sister only every second year, but that was better than never seeing her again. Elinor did not understand Judith's reluctance to marry. She herself had been taken from her family at age nine, had been married at twelve, and had given birth at fourteen. Aye, Norbert was neither young nor handsome, but what other choice did a maid have? Elinor thought of her son, John, now a toddler, and shook her head. She breathed deeply, still clutching the child in her womb. She must not upset herself or make herself sick. Women had lost babies for less.

Judith stroked her sister's fair hair, moved. "I am so sorry, dear Elinor, to distress you."

Elinor looked up. "Does that mean there will be no more shameful talk of running away?"

Judith removed her hand from Elinor's hair. "Nay. I still plan to go." She stared into her sister's eyes: blue eyes into blue eyes. Elinor looked away first.

"You'll be killed, and I shall never see you again."

"We shall meet in Heaven, then," Judith said, smiling. "If I marry Lord Norbert, we shall never see one another, either, dear sister. He will not let me far from home, I know. He does not let his five daughters leave the manor."

Elinor sighed, defeated. "How will you protect yourself on the way to Kent? 'Tis a journey of near two hundred miles."

Judith contained herself—she knew that a whoop of joy would alert Molly and send her running into the chamber. Instead, she clapped her hands together and pranced around the room in a silent jig. Elinor watched, amused despite herself. Judith was only two years younger than she, but Elinor had always felt more like the girl's mother. Even as a young child Judith had been like that, unable to hide her emotions, jubilantly happy or in utter despair, rarely in between.

When Judith had finished her dance, she threw herself into the cushioned chair next to Elinor and breathed, "I shall not go as the Lady Judith of Nesscliff, stepdaughter of Lord Walter. I am not such a simpkin as that."

"Then who shall you be?"

"A minstrel's apprentice, perhaps, or a merchant's boy, or a lawyer's son traveling to his apprenticeship. I can be many, many people, Elinor."

"A boy?" Elinor laughed. "How can you be a boy?" She gestured at Judith's waist-length golden hair and her delicate features.

"With short hair and a man's tunic and cape, who would know? I can say I am a youth and that way explain my lack of beard."

"Short hair?" Elinor was dismayed. Elinor prized

her own gold hair more highly than any jewel. A woman's hair was her crown.

But Judith seemed not to notice. She nodded, saying, "Aye, you must cut it before I leave. We can use a sharpened knife from the kitchen."

Elinor shuddered at the thought but questioned Judith further. "Where shall you find men's clothing the proper size? Geoffrey's and Henry's clothes are much too small," she said of their younger stepbrothers. "And Edmund took all his garments to the monastery. An adult's would be much too big, tall though you are."

"There are some clothes of Stephen's in the large trunk in our mother's chamber," Judith answered solemnly. Both girls still deeply mourned the death of their eldest brother.

Brushing off the sadness, Elinor nodded. Her logical mind continued to go over the various items Judith would need for such a long journey. "Do you have any coins?"

Soberly, Judith thought. "Nay. I shall have to bring something to sell in town."

Elinor said nothing, but she thought of her brimming jewel box. Surely there was something she could give her sister that her husband would not miss. "When shall you go?"

"As soon as I possibly can." Judith looked around

the chamber, at the familiar furniture and tapestries, as if already saying good-bye. "The night after next. I must arrange clothing and food and discover how to take a horse."

"A horse! You will definitely be caught if you take one of Lord Walter's horses, and whipped for a thief as well."

"Only until I am far enough away so they cannot find me. Then I can sell the horse. And I won't take one of Lord Walter's horses; I shall take one of Lord Norbert's." Her blue eyes glinted dangerously. " 'Tis the least he owes me, after all he is making me endure."

Judith lurked, waiting for her mother and the gentlewomen to leave Lady Cecilia's chamber for the stroll around the grounds her mother almost always took in clement weather. It was the only time of day Lady Cecilia's chamber was empty. As soon as Judith saw them enter the rose garden, she crept into the chamber and opened one of the enormous wooden trunks, her muscles straining to lift the heavy lid. But she was rewarded by the contents: breeches and tunics and a long traveling cloak, long pointed boots and a wide leather belt. With gratitude she saw that Stephen's fire kit—an oiled leather bag for holding flint and tinder—also lay within. Judith gathered up as many of her brother's possessions as she could carry, carefully shut the trunk, and scrambled back to her chamber, where Elinor was waiting.

Unfortunately, Molly was waiting, too. Judith burst into the room, clutching the pile of garments, and was brought up short by the sight of her maid, standing in the middle of the chamber.

"What are ye lasses up to, playing dress-up?" Molly asked, her eagle eye moving back and forth between Judith, holding the bundle of Stephen's clothes, and Elinor, who had all her jewels laid out on the dressing table.

Judith agonized for a moment. It would be nice to confide in another person, she thought; Molly had always seemed more a playmate than a servant. But what if she told . . . or, even worse, what if she was questioned, after Judith went away? Molly could be tortured, perhaps even killed.

"Aye, we're planning a pantomime!" Judith exclaimed with a big smile, striding over to the bed and dumping her bundle on it. "It's going to be a surprise, for Midsummer Eve." Judith sat down on the bed and crossed her arms, pretending now to be disappointed. "But you won't be surprised anymore—now you know!" She pulled her face down into a sulk.

"But Lady Judith, you'll be wed by . . . Nay, child, never mind. It is a nice thing to do. I'll be surprised as any, now, you'll see." She headed for the door. "You have your fun; I'll be in your mother's chamber if you need me to sew anything for your pantomime." She disappeared, shutting the door behind her.

Elinor looked at her sister with new respect. "That was clever." For the first time, she saw the possibility of Judith's actually carrying out this dangerous scheme.

By the next night, all was ready. Judith said good-bye, in her own fashion, to her family and the servants. She gave her mother an extra kiss when Lady Cecilia called her into her chamber; she patted each of her young stepbrothers on the head and slipped them sweetmeats from the grown-ups' table. She told Elinor to give Molly all the gowns that Elinor herself didn't want. Judith did nothing different, however, with Lord Walter or Lord Norbert. They were the reason she was running away. She tried to tell herself that she would have gone anyway, to pursue her music and a life of more freedom, but she knew that was a lie. If she were betrothed to a man she liked, she would not have been leaving.

Judith and Elinor both knew that Tobiah, the old groom, would be sound asleep by midnight, and the stable boys would be gone until dawn. Judith had gone down to the stables earlier, ostensibly to have a chat with the groom, but actually to decide which of Lord Norbert's horses she wanted to take. She picked out a black mare, gentle but strong. Her name was Sheba.

Judith's new traveling clothes were hidden under

her bed, ready to be put on at a moment's notice. A pack was filled: an extra tunic and pair of breeches; the fire kit, filled with raw wool for starting tinder; a sack of bread and hard cheese, dried salt pork, and some traveling cakes with dried fruits and nuts; a flask of ale and a small wooden bowl and cup. She had no room for her prayerbook, nor for any musical instrument besides the small pipes left by Robin. The few pennies Elinor had procured for Judith, as well as a silver bracelet set with garnets, which Elinor had never worn much, were tucked safely into a pouch that Judith would wear inside her tunic. There was also a short knife to wear on her belt. Elinor protested—she didn't want her sister carrying a knife—but Judith insisted that any traveler without a knife would be an easy target. She would teach herself how to use it.

A flash of metal glinted in the candlelight. Elinor stood before her sister, sharp steel scissors in hand. She had lifted them from Molly's sewing basket earlier and concealed them under the bedclothes.

Looking with pain at her sister's lovely golden hair, Elinor explained, "I thought these would do better than a kitchen knife. Is your mind settled, dear Judith?"

"Call me Jude. Remember, I am a boy now," was her answer.

Judith—Jude—sat stony-faced and still as Elinor, tears running down her cheeks, cut and snipped away at the gold locks until the nape of her sister's neck was bare and several feet of blond hair lay on the stone floor. Then Elinor laid the scissors down and heaved an exhausted sigh, turning her face away. She couldn't bear to look at her shorn sister.

Judith felt all over her head, getting used to the new sensation of short hair. It curled around her face, and she smiled to herself as she pushed the short tendrils behind her ears. *I really am Jude now,* she thought, and felt her old self slipping away as this new, courageous identity took its place.

Her heart pounding with excitement, Jude lay down on her bed, waiting for the rest of the manor's occupants to sleep. There wasn't a banquet or a feast, so everyone should be retiring early, but she had to be careful about Lord Walter, who sometimes paced throughout the rooms in the middle of the night. These days, he rarely went to his wife's chamber; she was often too ill for him to visit.

Elinor paced the chamber, too disturbed to rest. Suddenly she exclaimed, "Judith!"

"Jude!" her sister corrected.

Exasperated, Elinor replied, "Whether your name is Judith or Jude, we have a problem. What will we do with all this hair? We can't burn it—the smell would bring the whole manor in here."

Nodding, Jude sat up, her eyes roving around the chamber for a solution. She hadn't thought about how difficult it might be to get rid of a three-foot mane of hair. Any obvious hiding place would be discovered by Molly within the day, and then all would know what she had done. Jude was counting on escaping and going unnoticed as a boy; however, if Lord Walter launched a thorough search of the countryside for a short-haired girl in disguise, her chance of escape would be slim indeed.

When Jude's eyes settled on the decorative square Elinor had finished embroidering that morning, her face broke into a wide grin. "Do you have silk backing for that pillow, sister?" she asked casually.

"Aye, and linen rags for stuffing," Elinor answered slowly, not understanding her sister's smile.

Jude knelt on the floor and swept up the collection of gold hair. "I think you will be needing less linen for your pillow," she said, holding up the pile.

Elinor grimaced and then nodded reluctantly, reaching for her needle box. She was accomplished at fine sewing, and it did not take her long to attach three sides of the delicate embroidery to a blue silk square. Working together, the sisters rolled up the length of hair inside the clean linen rags and stuffed the little pillow full. Jude pressed the edges down as Elinor stitched up the fourth side. Then, satisfied with her solution and their quick work, Jude blew out the candles and lay down again to wait.

Perched at the foot of the bed, Elinor ran her hands

nervously along the seams of the pillow. It was not only her sister's ingenuity that amazed Elinor, but also her daring. Where had little Judith gotten so much courage? "Jude," Elinor corrected herself in a whisper. Had Elinor asked, she would have received the answer that Jude wasn't brave at all; she was merely acting for her survival.

"All seems quiet," Jude whispered into the silence. Much time had passed since she'd last heard any noise from the other occupants of the manor. "It is time." Rising silently from the bed, she started to assemble her clothes. She dressed by moonlight, not chancing to call any attention to herself by lighting a candle. She pulled on the breeches, boots, and tunic, then covered her newly shorn head with the hood of her short traveling cape.

Elinor waited anxiously, watching the dark shape of her sister move silently around the chamber.

Finally Jude stood in front of Elinor, fully dressed and pack in hand. "Come," she whispered, taking Elinor's hand. Elinor gently placed the pillow on the bed, the design standing out against the duller linens.

The two sisters opened the door of the chamber and listened intently. Silence. Jude then shut the door and padded softly to the main staircase, the one that led down to the great hall. She would have preferred using one of the back stairs, those leading to the kitchen and storerooms, but servants slept in the downstairs chambers. She would not chance discovery.

They crept down the huge stone staircase, pausing every few steps to listen. When they reached the great hall, Jude veered off to the right, pulling Elinor with her. Elinor started but didn't say a word. She understood when Jude steered them both to the largest metal shield in a row of armor that dominated one wall of the hall. By the moonlight shining in through one of the casements, Elinor could just make out their distorted forms, reflected in the polished shield. She inhaled sharply, shaking her head in disbelief. The reflection showed her, in her white dressing gown, standing next to her dead brother Stephen.

Of course, it wasn't Stephen. But Judith, in that costume, was the very image of their brother at age eleven or twelve. Jude, herself struck dumb, removed the hood, and Elinor shook her head. The resemblance was even closer when Jude's hair wasn't covered. At least in the moonlight, Jude could pass for a boy.

What Jude would do in broad daylight, Elinor didn't ask. Or what would happen if she started her monthly bleeding, or if her breasts grew large. Right now, Jude's tiny breasts were bound with a tight linen band, but that would not work if she suddenly matured. Elinor raised her hand to her own well-developed bosom and saw in the mirror her rounded torso. She was with child, after all; 'twas not surprising that she was twice her sister's size. But the contrast still amazed her.

Jude smiled in the mirror, as if she knew exactly what her sister was thinking. Slowly she replaced the traveling hood and took Elinor's hand again. Jude was delighted with her reflection. She'd had several waves of panic earlier, thinking that the costume wouldn't work, that she would look as silly as the men who dressed as maidens for the Twelfth Night pantomimes. But she could put her mind at rest now. This would come right, after all.

And then they were at the manor doors. It took both of them to slide back the large bar and open the heavy door. Elinor worried that she would not be able to push the bar back by herself. *I can ask one of the servants to help,* she decided. *I can tell them I came down for some bread and cheese—I am feeding two, now—and discovered the door was unbarred.* For Lord Walter would be mightily angered if the doors were unbarred when he awoke, and she couldn't leave the manor so unprotected for the rest of the night.

When they stood in the doorway, in the night air, Elinor felt the pricking of tears in her eyes. She kissed her sister on both cheeks, then placed her hands on Jude's shoulders, whispering, "Fare thee well, Judith . . . Jude. Godspeed."

"May we meet again, under kinder circumstances,"

Jude whispered back, barely controlling her own tears. She kissed her sister and turned to go.

Elinor waved, and whispered again, to Jude's retreating back, "Use care, my beloved sister, and may God protect you."

"May God have you in his keeping," Jude replied. She waved and then disappeared into the night.

IV

INTO THE WOODS

That night, Jude and Sheba, the black horse, were able to travel for only three or four hours before dawn broke. They did not cover as much ground as Jude had hoped. She had pictured them riding away at top speed, outrunning all Lord Walter's soldiers, but picking their way through the forest made for slow going. Jude couldn't risk taking one of the roads, for fear of discovery. If she was found by a stranger, she had her story in place: she would say she was from a nearby town, making her way to Bridgenorth to be a page. That was where Stephen had been trained. It was such a short distance, her father had sent her alone, but she had gotten lost in the woods. Of course, she was a boy. If she was somehow discovered to be a girl and escorted back to Nesscliff,

50

she would need to think of another plan. But right now, she just hoped to find a hiding place for the day.

It was unpleasant traveling alone at night; Jude hadn't counted on that. Often the terrain in the forest was so rocky and obscure she had to get down and lead the horse. She lost a lot of time that way and wasn't nearly far enough away from her stepfather's manor to feel safe. The peasants in the nearby cottages were Lord Walter's tenants; anyone who found her would be duty bound to turn her in.

So, where can a girl hide herself and a large black horse in the forest in the daylight? Jude thought. She was exhausted and not thinking clearly. As the sky turned orange, then pink, then blue through the trees, the thought of turning around and going back home crossed her mind. She shook her head violently. Going back home would mean going back to Lord Norbert. She pressed on through the woods, Sheba in tow.

Jude stopped in a dark clearing overhung with trees and sheltered by large boulders. She listened, and once she was satisfied that no one was near, she removed Sheba's bridle and let the horse graze. Jude dropped to the ground, exhausted by lack of sleep and the fear that was gnawing at her. She opened her pack and took out a thick slice of bread with cheese. The crust was a bit crumbled and the cheese dusty from the clothes in her pack, but she gobbled it down anyway. A good swig of ale finished her meal. With a sigh, she settled back against a boulder. Not the most comfortable of resting spots, but it would do for now. She'd just close her eyes for a moment. . . .

She awoke suddenly, her heart racing. Where was she? What hour of the day was it? She got to her feet, shaking her head to clear the fogginess she felt in her mind. "Sheba," she called softly, and the horse trotted out of the woods back to her. Jude heaved a relieved sigh, thankful that her transportation hadn't decided to abandon her and go back to the manor. Jude wrapped her arms around the horse's neck, scratching her mane. Sheba snorted with delight and nuzzled Jude's ear with her big wet nose. Jude giggled and said aloud, "I've never been so glad to see a horse before!"

She clapped her hand over her mouth—her voice sounded strange. She looked around; luckily, there was no one to hear. Only witches and lunatics spoke to animals, she knew, and she certainly didn't want to be mistaken for either of those. However, one did speak to animals when training them: teaching oxen to move left or right, or falcons to hunt, or horses to speed up or slow down. "I'm just training you," she whispered to Sheba, petting the horse behind her ears. It felt good to be talking to someone, if only a horse. Jude was not used to being alone. During her days at the convent and the manor, she had always been surrounded by people.

Looking up at the sun overhead, Jude knew that it

was around noon. She stood, undecided about what to do next. If she traveled farther in daylight, she might be discovered. Then again, she might be found even if she stayed in this clearing. With an uneasy sigh, she bridled Sheba again and slung on her own pack. Mounting with a swift, practiced motion, she nudged the mare to start walking slowly through the woods again.

Every few minutes, however, she stopped Sheba to listen and get her bearings in the woods. She hadn't yet articulated her plan, not even to herself, but in the back of her mind was the idea that she would make her way southeast to London and then continue in the same direction to Eltham Palace. In London she could sell Sheba and the garnet bracelet Elinor had given her, stock up on provisions, and find out the best way to reach Kent. Perhaps in some tavern she could hear which roads were likely to be plagued by bandits and which were protected by the King's guards. If only she could make it to London; Walter certainly wouldn't find her there. Jude knew she might be able to stop safely in one of the smaller, closer cities, like Warwick or Bedford, but somehow London beckoned her; she had never been there, but it sounded so large and so crowded it must be easy to be anonymous there.

Toward dusk, she was riding along the edge of a steep drop, with a stream running below in the crevice. Suddenly she noticed Sheba prick up her ears and give a soft snort. Jude stopped the horse and slid down, all her senses alert. They were in the forest. She could hear them calling, faintly, far off yet, but coming closer. She heard hounds with them and knew that she and the horse could never outrun a hunting pack, not through this dense wood. Her heart pounding, she grabbed Sheba's reins and started to lead the mare down the incline.

Sheba balked, but Jude pulled her along with a steady hand, sending silent thanks to whichever of Norbert's grooms had trained the docile animal. They picked their way down the rocks, sending dust and pebbles cascading below. At one point, Sheba slipped, skidding a few feet. Jude, panicking, felt tears starting to stream down her face. If Sheba fell and broke a leg . . . Jude banished the thought from her mind. It never occurred to her that *she* might fall and break something; all her concern was for the horse—and for not being caught.

When they finally reached the bottom of the ledge, Jude choked back relieved sobs. Barely pausing for breath, she pulled Sheba into the stream. It was their only chance—the dogs couldn't follow a scent through water. The stream, ice-cold even in late spring, was flowing swiftly, but Jude plunged in without hesitation. She sucked in her breath as the frigid water soaked first through her boots, then her breeches, then the bottom part of her tunic. She just hoped that the water wouldn't reach her pack. She couldn't carry the pack in her arms while leading Sheba, and though the horse was obedient, Jude doubted she would follow through the icy water without being led.

Jude was shivering when they finally reached the other side. Sheba wasn't any happier. The mare gave an unhappy neigh and sank to the ground, starting to roll in the earth to dry off. Jude watched, horrified, listening to the approaching hounds. She couldn't even pull at the reins with Sheba rolling around like that.

"What's the matter, lad, yer horse misbehaving?"

Jude jumped, then turned to see an old woman standing behind her. She now noticed a small straw-roofed cottage off to the side, with a neat vegetable garden, some chickens, and two goats in a pen. The woman wore a brown surcoat and a white apron; though very old, she looked at Jude with clear gray eyes.

Jude opened her mouth to answer, but no sound came out. Wordlessly she pointed up to the ledge. The woman listened for a moment, heard the hunting dogs, and gave Jude a push toward the cottage. "Go dry yourself by the fire," she said. "I'll deal with the animal." The woman clicked her tongue twice, bringing Sheba up from the ground. She took the reins and started to lead the horse away. "G'wan." She nodded to the little hut. "Get yourself in there." Jude didn't need to be told again.

Thinking about it later, Jude had no idea why she had trusted the strange old woman. If she had been one of Walter's tenants, she would have been obligated to turn Jude in. But she had felt safe with the woman; somehow, seeing her handle Sheba with such total confidence, she knew that the woman wasn't bound by the same laws as the peasants and serfs, who always seemed frightened by her stepfather and his men. This old crone didn't seem frightened at all.

As for the old woman, with one glance she took in Jude's tear-streaked face and trembling body. She didn't need to think twice about helping this poor, wet child. For with the breeches and tunic plastered against her body, even the tight binding around her small breasts couldn't completely hide Jude's figure, and the old woman was curious. First she would tend to the horse; then she would find out what the little thing was up to and why she was dressed as a boy.

Jude entered the small cottage hesitantly, opening the door and letting her eyes adjust to the soft light inside the whitewashed space. The hut had only one room, with a sleeping cot by one wall and a sturdy wooden table against the other, and a large fireplace with a cauldron and spit hanging over it on the far side, across from the door. It smelled mossy and pleasant inside, so Jude took a few steps in. Bunches of plants hung upside down on a wooden rack by the fire, and the dirt floor was strewn with rushes and sweet herbs. One of the chickens followed her in, but Jude shooed her out again, mindful of the clean floor. She walked over to the fire and stood, waiting for the old woman. The fire needed tending, so she stirred it with an iron poker and placed another log on top, but still the woman didn't return. Jude didn't know what to do, so she just stood there, shivering, grateful for the warming fire.

"There now," the woman's voice came from the doorway. She shut and bolted the wooden door. "Yer horse is tucked away safely, happy as can be. I gave her some hay to keep her quiet." She turned and faced Jude. "Now, let's get you out of those wet clothes . . . lad. Do you have a spare set, or do I need to lend you a gown?" Her eyes twinkled as she asked.

Something about her look, and the way she said "lad," made Jude know that the woman wasn't deceived. With a rueful sigh, Jude stripped off her wet clothes in full view of the woman and stepped into the dry ones from her pack. Chuckling, the old woman wrung out the dripping garments and hung them on a line by the fire. She took two wooden bowls down from the mantelpiece, dished pottage from the cauldron into them and motioned for Jude to join her at the table.

As the woman ducked her head and moved her lips, saying a silent grace, Jude too bowed her head and offered words of thanks, realizing in the midst of her prayers how ravenously hungry she was. The fright of almost being discovered was gone, and she could now feel the empty rumbling in the pit of her stomach. Then, after waiting to see that it was all right to start, she dug hungrily into the stew with a wooden spoon the woman had placed in front of her. Jude would have eaten anything, she was so hungry, but the pottage was truly delicious—thick with beef and root vegetables, seasoned with parsley, onions, and cress. Jude wondered where the woman had gotten such good meat, but she didn't dare to ask. They ate in silence, sharing goat's milk out of a wooden cup.

When they had finished the meal, the woman got up from the table and went over to the corner of the hut, rummaging through some cloth sacks that stood neatly on the floor. She pulled out two small apples, then spoke. "One for us, and one for yer pretty horse. Now, lass, tell me what brings you here."

Jude had sworn, before she left her stepfather's manor, that she would keep her secrets to herself. She would be a person of mystery to those who met her. But all those resolutions were thrown to the wind when the old woman asked her to speak. It was more of a command, really, and for some reason Jude could not resist. Her story came pouring out as the woman cut the apple with a sharp knife and placed the slices between the two of them on the table. Jude gobbled up her half of the delicious fruit while talking, not caring about her mother's strict rule of not talking with one's mouth full; Jude sensed that the old woman didn't much care for courtly manners.

When both the story and the apple were done, Jude said to the woman, "And I thought I could make it all the way to Kent as a boy. But here you are, the first person I meet, and you knew at once that I was not male." Jude felt foolish that she had been discovered so quickly, but the cottage was warm and her belly was full, so she didn't mind so terribly at the moment. Actually, she just felt surprisingly sleepy. She yawned, waiting for an answer.

The old woman smiled at her, crinkling up the already wrinkled skin around her deep gray eyes. "Don't you worry about that, lass. I see more than most people do. Comes from living alone. Now, get you off to bed." She gestured to the cot against the wall. "I'll see to your horse."

Unable to resist, Jude stumbled over to the straw-stuffed cot and lay down. It was small and lumpy compared to her bed at home, but much superior to lying in the forest, against a rock. She was asleep before she could even pull the covers up over her shoulders, so the old woman did that for her before going out to see to Sheba.

Maybe it was the relief of feeling safe again after the terrible night of travel, or the good, hearty food eaten with ravenous hunger. Or maybe it was something the old woman put in the stew; but, for whatever reason, Jude slept like a babe throughout that evening and night and well into the next morning. When she woke, she sat up in confusion, unable to understand where she was, then relaxed when she saw the woman sitting in one of the wooden chairs, placidly mending an apron.

"Ah, so yer finally awake, lass. I thought you'd sleep the day away." Her eyes twinkled at Jude.

Jude's hands flew up to her face. "Oh, I took your bed! I apologize most humbly!" She was mortified at her lack of manners. What would Lady Cecilia think of her? On the other hand, what would her mother think if she knew that her daughter was roaming the countryside dressed as a boy and sleeping in peasants' cottages?

The woman seemed unconcerned about any of those things. She chuckled and said, "Don't you mind, dear. I don't need so much sleep as a young thing like you. Now we must get you ready for the next bit of your journey."

"Thank you for your help." Jude got out of the small cot and stood before the woman. "I don't know what I would have done if you hadn't been here."

The woman gave a curt nod and answered, "You'll always have something or someone to help when you need it, girl. I can see it in your eyes. Yer meant to make this trip to the King's palace, so you'll get there, don't you worry." She said this seriously, her hands all the while sewing tiny stitches on the apron.

Jude had a moment of panic—was this woman a witch?—before relaxing again. *No, she's just a wise old crone who likes to tell tales,* she assured herself.

The wise crone saw the changes in Jude's eyes and chuckled once more. "Let's get you some food, lass, and then make a plan."

They breakfasted on bread and goat's milk cheese, and the woman then drew a crude but clear map on a scrap of parchment. "Until yer out of Lord Walter's land, and that neighboring his, you must keep traveling by night. So, another night in the woods, then you'll be safe, at least from his men." She sketched the forest and the road with a blackened piece of wood from the fire. "Stay away from the main southern road until you get to the outskirts of London, and the minor roads, too. They're beset with bandits and thieves. Yer belt knife wouldn't help much against a gang o' them."

Jude nodded, again scared by the journey ahead of her. The woman patted her hand and got up from the chair, moving toward the bunches of herbs hanging by the fire. For an old woman, Jude thought, she stepped remarkably lightly.

The woman placed handfuls of herbs on the wooden table, then searched the small cottage until she had found several scraps of clean cloth. As Jude watched intently, the woman mixed herbs and powders, then poured them into three different cloths. "This," she said, pointing to the first mixture, which lay on a white cloth, "use this in the water you drink from streams. Only drink water that runs clear, but even that can be dirty and cause sickness. Mix a pinch of this powder in, stir well, and wait a minute or two before drinking. Promise me you'll do it!" She looked at Jude so seriously, that the girl had to nod, agreeing. Jude didn't want to admit that she'd not thought about what she would drink when her ale was finished. The old woman continued, pointing to the second mixture, spread out on a brown cloth. "This one is if you feel ill or melancholy on yer trip. Twice a day, mix a palmful with hot, clear water and drink it all down." She bound these two mixtures tightly and handed them to Jude. "This one is more dangerous." She lowered her voice as she spoke about the third mixture, which lay on a scrap of black cloth. "Use it if you need to gain mastery over an enemy or an attacker. You must find a way to put a palmful of this in his drink. It will not kill him, but rather weaken him enough to give you time for escape."

Jude looked uncertainly at the mixture, asking cautiously, "What powerful herbs are those?"

"Opium and hemlock," the woman replied gravely. "Use it only when *utterly* necessary." Carefully she tied the scrap of cloth with a series of knots and handed it to Jude. The girl placed the three small bundles in her sack, along with the map the woman had sketched.

"How do you know so much about herbs?" Jude asked, trying to keep suspicion out of her voice.

The old woman laughed. "I'm the midwife round these parts, and also a healer for them who can't afford a real physician. I trade herbs and midwifery for food, not coins. That's where my bread and meat come from, most times."

Jude nodded—the woman had such a calming air about her, she could see her birthing infants and soothing the sick, even taking care of animals. Animals!

"Sheba?" Jude asked with sudden panic.

"The horse is fine; don't you worry, dear. She's grazing happily with a few other horses at the farm downstream a bit. I left her covered with mud so no one could tell what a black beauty she is. You really should have picked a less striking horse, my lass, a spotted brown, perhaps, like are all around the countryside."

Jude hung her head with shame. It had not occurred to her that Sheba's beautiful coloring would be a problem.

"Now, don't you worry, dear, we'll get you safely to London, then on to Kent. 'Tis in the stars, it is," the woman said mysteriously, but Jude didn't ask what she meant. She didn't really want to know.

That afternoon, Jude curried Sheba, brushing off all the caked mud and covering her with a brown blanket.

At least from a distance, then, the horse did not look so different from the other animals. Jude rolled her now dry breeches and tunic and packed them up, and oiled her boots until they were soft again. The old woman served a filling meal of eggs and strips of salt bacon, and the two sat at the table, drinking buttermilk, until the dark surrounded them.

Jude's eyes stung as she strapped on her pack, and she tried not to cry. It was harder to leave this old woman than it had been her own sister; mostly, she knew, because she now understood how difficult the traveling would be, in a way she had not two nights before.

"God bless you," Jude said, clutching the woman in a tight embrace. "You rescued me. And I don't even know what your name is."

"Everyone calls me Goodwife Middy, child. I have two things to remind you; then you'll be on yer way. Be careful how you use the third powder, because it's very potent. And don't doubt that you'll get to Kent; it's written in the stars. God bless you and keep you safe."

And with that, she gave Jude a final hug and sent her out the door, into the clear night.

V

PERCIVAL

*T*he second night of traveling was easier than the
first, but Jude still spent the hours with a knot
of fear in her stomach and the blood pounding in her
ears. The near-capture had frightened her terribly, and
she jumped at every sound in the forest. Again, she
rode Sheba only part of the time; over rocky territory
or land so shaded by thick trees that moonlight didn't
penetrate, she led the obedient horse. *I may not have
picked the right color animal,* Jude thought, *but at least I
found one with the right temper.*

Stopping in a dense thicket at daybreak, Jude studied the map Goodwife Middy had sketched. It seemed
that Jude was already in the territory of a different
lord. Pleased, she unbridled Sheba and brushed down
the tired horse, speaking softly to her and feeding her

one of Goodwife Middy's small apples as a treat. She let the horse graze and hunkered down to eat one of her traveling cakes. As the sun rose into the sky, Jude gave a soft whistle for Sheba, who came trotting back.

"Now, you stay by me," Jude told the horse. There was plenty of grass to eat surrounding the thicket, and she did not want the animal wandering too far off. Jude laid herself down among the shrubs, obscured from the view of anyone who wasn't passing directly next to her. The ground was damp and chilly, with small stones and twigs Jude kept brushing away from underneath her. She pulled her traveling cloak tighter around her shoulders and willed the weak morning sun to warm her a bit. Then she slept, despite the chill and the daylight and the hard bed.

Waking briefly when the sun was directly overhead, she checked to make sure Sheba was still near and rolled back into a deep sleep. It was midafternoon before she woke again, but this time she sat up, fully alert, sensing danger.

She heard a loud squawk, then another. Soon she located the source of the noise: a medium-sized peregrine falcon, perched on a low branch directly above her. For a moment she thought, *Oh, it's only a bird,* and relaxed, but then, with surprise, she recognized it. It was Lord Walter's prize falcon, the one that always rode on his forearm.

Scrambling to her feet, she seized a nearby rock,

took aim, and threw. She brought the falcon down with that one blow. It fell, soundlessly, the short drop to the ground, and Jude scooped it up in her arms and huddled in the thicket.

The bird's small heart was beating wildly, and a steady stream of blood trickled from the wound on its head. "Poor birdie," she muttered, even though the bird would have exposed Jude to her pursuers.

Jude heard a neigh of fright and remembered with a start that Sheba was nearby. Panic momentarily clouded her mind, but she shook off the creeping webs of fear and got to work. The plan she had suddenly thought of was crazy, but so was her entire journey.

She soundlessly opened her sack and pulled out her spare tunic. Tearing off a strip of soft cloth, she mopped as much blood as she could from the wounded bird; then, leaving the falcon in the thicket, she crept on her belly to where Sheba was grazing. She couldn't yet hear Walter and his men but knew they would not be far behind.

Stealthily Jude got to her feet, first peering around to make sure she wasn't being watched. Then she laid the blood-spotted rag lightly across Sheba's back. It wouldn't stay on for long, but that suited her plan. Whispering to the horse, she led her in the direction of the woods whence she had come, gave her a hug around the neck and said good-bye. She whacked Sheba across the rump and sent her trotting into the forest. Then Jude made her way back to the shrub with her sack and the poor bird and sat, waiting.

It was likely that Walter would come looking for his falcon. And if he still had the hunting dogs with him, he would find Jude. Her only hope was that the horse and the bloodstained tunic would make him think she was dead. He probably wished she were dead, Jude reasoned; maybe this would make it easier to believe.

But what about the falcon? Jude had thought she could just leave it in the forest; maybe Walter would think the same animal that had attacked *her* had also got the falcon. But Jude felt her heart go out to the poor animal. Perhaps because she'd had to sacrifice Sheba, her only companion, she felt sympathetic to this injured creature. She pulled a clean strip of cloth from her bag—an extra one Goodwife Middy had given her to use as a bandage—and bound the falcon's wound. The cloth covered the bird's eyes, but that was all right; Walter usually kept the falcon hooded when it was not hunting.

Torn between staying in the thick brush and trying to outrun her stepfather, Jude decided to keep moving. Better to be caught running than cornered in the thicket. She bundled her pack on her back, cradling the falcon in her arms, and set off to the south.

Traveling like that was unspeakably difficult, carrying a bulky bird and a heavy sack and moving in a half-crouch so as to be less visible to her pursuers. Jude paused often, sinking down against the trees to catch her breath. It had been hard going through the woods leading Sheba, but at least the horse had carried her pack. Jude thought sadly of Sheba but knew there was no way she could have kept the horse and escaped discovery. A youth and a medium-sized falcon were easy enough to spot; a youth and a horse were impossible to miss.

Jude's third day of travel passed in a blur. She paused only to get her bearings and to check on the injured bird, about which she suddenly cared a great deal. *I hope it doesn't die,* she thought. *And I wish I could remember its name.*

Toward dusk, when she stopped to rest, she heard the hunting dogs again. She was back on her feet in an instant, tearing through the woods, holding the still bird high to avoid catching it in the brush. Jude had been traveling almost parallel to the stream, and now she moved toward its icy waters again. The dogs were some distance off, she knew, but their howling still sent chills down her spine. She paused at the edge of the stream. She'd learned her lesson last time. This time, she knew, there'd be no old woman on the other side at whose fire she could warm herself. Hurriedly she stripped off her boots and stuffed them in her sack. Then she rolled up her breeches as far as they'd go. Taking the breeches off crossed her mind, but what if she was discovered? The added humiliation of being caught half-naked would be more than she could endure. So she just rolled the cloth until it was over her knees and plunged into the swift, cold water.

The water stung her bare feet, and sharp stones stabbed them. Jude cradled the bird in her arms, trying not to lose her balance and drop the poor thing, which would easily be swept away by the current and drowned. Jude was shivering when she reached the steep bank on the far side of the stream, but she paused to listen. The dogs were coming closer. Hurrying, she pulled her boots onto her wet feet, which were almost blue with the cold, and scrambled farther upstream. Her numb feet stumbled frequently, but she plowed on. Then she stubbed her right foot against a large, protruding tree root and came to a halt. "By Mary!" she swore under her breath, laying the falcon down and holding her hurt foot. Tears sprang into her eyes, but she blinked them away, looking over her shoulder. Still no one in sight. She looked ahead and caught her breath: the enormous willow in front of her was weeping its leaves into the water of the stream; the leafy branches would provide a sheltered space, totally obscured from view. Grabbing the falcon once again, Jude scrambled between the branches to the space inside.

It was like her own private tent. She gave a smile of delight, and, one-handed, clutching the bird to her chest with the other, she hauled herself up into the crook of the tree's branches. Perched well above the ground, she was satisfied that no passersby would discern her. Especially from the other side of the water, downstream . . .

"Percival!" she heard a man's voice calling. Her stepfather's voice. She shuddered and huddled closer to the bark of the tree. *"Percival!"* He was directly across the stream. Jude's mind was clouded with fear, but she thought, *Who is Percival?* and then remembered—the falcon. She hugged the animal closer to herself, determined that Walter wouldn't get it back.

Later it occurred to her to be hurt, then amused, that Walter searched harder for his falcon than for his stepdaughter, but at the time she merely held her breath and tried to think calming thoughts: of playing duets with Elinor, of sitting next to Gwynna at Mass in the convent. She recited silently all the Latin prayers she knew, and when she had finished with them, all the French ones. In the end, Walter and his hunting party never passed close to her willow tree; they stayed on the opposite side of the bank, first going far upstream, shouting for the falcon, then returning. Jude sat in the tree for the many hours it took them to abandon their search. Not until they had long since retreated and the night was fully dark did Jude carefully make her way down to the ground. That was the last she saw—or heard—of her stepfather.

As Jude's feet touched the ground again, her legs

hardly held her up. She sank down to her knees, drawing ragged breaths of relief. "O Merciful Lord Jesus Christ, never forsaking His servant in time of need, worshiped be His name, so blessed may He be," she intoned under her breath, her prayer of thanksgiving cut short only by exhaustion. She crept out from the protection of the willow branches only once, to scoop water from the stream into her wooden cup, then scurried back to cover. She sprinkled the herbs from Goodwife Middy's first bundle into the water, lay on the damp ground within the tree's circle of cover, and slept before the water was even ready to drink.

Jude woke to an aching thirst and a strange noise by her ear. She sat up, rubbing her eyes, and reached gratefully for the cup of water, which lay on the ground where she had left it. The falcon, Percival, voicing periodic caws of annoyance, was on his feet, butting his head against the tree trunk, trying to remove the bandage that covered his eyes.

Jude laughed out loud at the sight, then covered her mouth. She still needed to be quiet, she thought. "Some noble bird!" she whispered aloud, and went to remove the bandage. Carefully she unrolled the cloth from the bird's head, while Percival stood motionless on his thin yellow legs and dangerous-looking talons. Leaning over, she met the bird eye to eye. *"Kek-kek-*

kek!" Percival cried, launching himself upward and settling in a high branch of the willow.

Jude scrambled to her feet. "Don't fly away!" she called, heedless of the noise she was making. "I'll be kinder to you than my stepfather was. I promise!" Promises did not bring the animal back down. Jude opened her sack and pulled out the last of her salt meat. She held it up high, hoping to get the falcon's attention. He looked down at her, haughty and unmoving. Despondently she sat on the ground, laying the meat a few paces away. She chewed on a dry traveling cake and thought.

She remembered a story told by a minstrel at a banquet a long time ago, about charming an angry bear from attacking. She'd thought it was just a tall tale, but why not give it a try? She rummaged in her sack and pulled out the pipes Robin had left for her. *So convenient for traveling,* she thought again, *that he gave me the pipes, instead of his drum or lute.*

She placed her hands carefully on the little pipes, pausing a moment before starting a pretty tune, light and playful. It reminded her of birds' singing, and now she hoped the falcon would think so, too. Up and down she played, not daring to look at the bird. Let him think she was playing for her own pleasure.

And then the bird was next to her, pecking hungrily at the salt meat she'd left on the ground. Jude didn't dare stop playing. She continued her merry tune while watching the falcon out of the corner of her eye. When Percival had finished eating, he stayed beside her, cocking his head and watching her play. The two sat that way for a long time.

When Jude, out of breath and with aching lips and hands, finally put down her pipes, the falcon remained on the ground. Jude dared not move an inch. She finally spoke. "Are you going to stay with me, Percival?" she asked softly. The bird, of course, didn't answer. Jude tried again. "Will you let me pet you?" She slowly extended her hand to the bird. Percival tilted his head to the other side and watched cautiously. Then, with no warning, he gave a little hop, with a flap of his wings, and landed on Jude's shoulder.

Jude was delighted, even though the falcon was digging his knife-sharp talons into her shoulder. She remembered—too late—that her stepfather padded his forearm when taking Percival out. Sucking in her breath from the pain, but moving slowly so as not to disturb the bird, Jude pulled out more strips of cloth from her sack. She wound a bandage thickly around her forearm and coaxed the falcon down from her shoulder. She sighed in relief, holding her cut and bloodied left shoulder with her right hand, while Percival perched, unconcerned, on her left arm. She'd have to mend her tunic, since she'd torn her spare one and sent it off on Sheba's back. The falcon's talons had slashed the thick material. It never occurred to her that she might punish the bird for injuring her, or send him back into the woods. A falcon did what it was trained to do, and it was her own fault that she'd forgotten to pad her shoulder.

At least Percival was company for her. With Sheba gone, she would have been entirely on her own. Animal companionship was better than none, and she knew it would be weeks before she reached London and could speak with other people. Percival would do just fine for now.

VI

A ROOM AT THE INN

*A*fter the next full day passed without any sign of her stepfather and his men, Jude fell into a comfortable pattern of traveling during the daylight hours and sleeping at night. She made much better time that way; according to the rough map drawn by Goodwife Middy, she would be in London in a fortnight, or perhaps in three weeks if the terrain became especially rough.

Although she felt safer, she still carefully avoided other people. She skirted the small villages she passed and hid deep in the forest when she heard others nearby. She had several possible stories ready in case she did come in contact with another person, but she was content to wait until London to try them out. For the first time she was her own mistress. No convent rules or manor conventions to follow. She slept when tired, ate when hungry, and, when she was sure no one was near, she played her pipes and sang as loudly as she wished.

When her traveling food began to run out, she gathered her meals from the forest. As late spring turned to summer, berries were abundant, as were leafy greens and tubers. However, Jude stuck to familiar plants, having heard stories of pilgrims poisoning themselves in the woods with strange greens and mushrooms.

Around the time her last traveling cake had been eaten, Jude discovered another reason to be glad that she had kept Percival. She'd made a shoulder pad out of the last of Goodwife Middy's bandages and had taken to walking with him on her shoulder. She hadn't bothered to make a hood for the falcon, though, since he seemed content to stay close to her most of the time, occasionally launching himself into the air and circling the woods lazily before returning to his perch.

But one morning, at daybreak, Jude lay on her bed of leaves, trying to shake off the stiffness and chill that came from sleeping unprotected in the woods. Percival, who had been making his customary waking-up squawks, suddenly stopped, dead still, then launched himself into the air at top speed.

Jude bolted upright, catching her breath. "Percival!" She followed him with her eyes until he dropped out of sight among the trees. Scrambling to her feet, carelessly brushing off the leaves that stuck to her tunic, she scanned the air for her companion. Before she could panic, however, Percival was back, with a fat pigeon in his talons. He dropped to the ground with a victorious cry and started to eat the bird, tearing off the feathers with his hooked beak and then ripping the flesh apart with abandon.

Jude watched, first with queasy disgust at the bloody sight, then with the awareness that this might solve her dilemma. If Percival could hunt for the two of them . . .

The falcon was too tired and full to do anything but settle on Jude's shoulder and sleep the rest of the day, but Jude was forming a plan as she trekked through the forest. The trick would be to get the animal away from Percival before he ripped into it.

When Percival awoke at dusk, Jude had already set up her small camp, placing her sack on the ground and gathering soft leaves for her bed. She heard the usual birdcalls throughout the forest, truly aware of them for the first time. When a flock of thrushes passed over-head, Jude moved Percival down to her arm; then, mimicking the motion she'd seen her stepfather use, she launched the falcon into the air toward the other birds.

"Get me some supper!" Jude called softly as Percival swooped over the now frantic small birds, scattering them. In moments he was before Jude again, a dead

thrush in his talons. It was easier than Jude had anticipated to get the bird away from Percival; she guessed
he was still sated from his morning meal.

Jude's satisfaction at getting the thrush away from
Percival, however, was short-lived. She stared at the
dead bird in her hands, tears welling up in her eyes. It
looked so small and helpless with its broken neck. She
shot a glance at Percival, who was preening his feathers, altogether unaware of his mistress's sorrow. *How
can he do that?* Jude thought. *How can he just kill?* She
blinked away the tears then. "But I won't starve now,
will I, Percival?" At his name, the falcon looked up. "I
should be thankful, not disgusted." Shaking her head,
Jude knelt down and started plucking the feathers off
the little bird.

Once she'd crudely plucked and butchered the bird
with her belt knife, she had gone in search of dry
wood. Her search was hindered by the fact that she
had to carry the dead bird with her, fearful that Percival or some other forest animal would eat it if she left
it alone.

Getting the fire started had been quite a trial, taking
many attempts and provoking many curses and
thrown sticks. Jude had never made a fire before, but
she had watched her brother Stephen do it many times.
That was more than six years ago, of course, and
watching wasn't the same as doing, but the picture in
her mind was clear. After brushing away all the leaves

and needles from a circular patch of forest ground, she laid down the largest pieces of dried wood. She followed with smaller pieces, then twigs, then a few tufts of raw wool. By quickly dragging the flint from her kit along the rough steel edge of her belt knife, she produced a satisfying number of sparks. They all went out, though, for she had not thought to direct them onto her tinder. After many false starts with the flint and steel, she finally produced a large, glowing spark that ignited the wool. Dropping her face close to the tinder, she blew until the flame became hot and strong enough to consume the twigs. When the fire was truly lit, she let out a whoop of joy. She roasted the bird over the open fire, her mouth watering at the smell.

She had never had such a delicious meal. The thrush was half burnt, half undercooked, for she'd had to hold it over the fire on a stick, having failed to get a spit to stick in the ground. But her fire had stayed lit. She laughed out loud at the wonderful taste of the meat, at the facts that she had made her own fire, and that no one had caught her yet, and that her mother would have died right then if she could have seen her youngest daughter eating with less manners than a serf. The small bird did little to quench her appetite, but Jude was happy when she finally closed her eyes that night.

The days blurred together as Jude continued to travel southeast. She walked at a steady pace through the woods, skirting towns and crossing an occasional full stream. When it rained she sought the shelter of a large tree or overhanging boulder or just plodded along. Often she sang to Percival as they walked. Her boots and breeches were caked with mud, and she hadn't bathed since she left Walter's manor, but there was no one in the woods to see how coarse she looked, and besides, Jude didn't care. She was far, far away from her mother and the nuns.

Some habits, however, ran too deep to be ignored. Jude tried to follow the days so that she could fast on Fridays—not completely, but avoiding meat and saying extra prayers. But without nuns or clergy around to keep the calendar, she could not remember the saints' days. Guiltily she knew that the Feast of St. John the Baptist was approaching, or perhaps had already passed. The nagging feeling came again toward the end of June; to appease her conscience, she said more fervent prayers, and wished she knew the exact day of the feast of St. Peter and St. Paul.

When she caught a mild cold, she holed up for one day in a dry crevice of rocks that lay piled near the streambed. She made a fire and heated stones. Then using two sticks to pick them up, she dropped them into water in her wooden bowl. When the water was hot, she sprinkled in some of the herb concoction Goodwife Middy had given her—the one from the brown cloth, which the old woman had said would be good for illness or melancholy. As she drank the warm mixture, Jude identified barley and licorice among other unfamiliar tastes. She was glad of the hot drink, of the medicinal herbs, and most of all the daily catch Percival brought her. That was now part of their pattern: the falcon would deposit a bird for Jude every evening, and Jude would stroke him with gratitude. The falcon seemed to love the friendly attention; Jude could only guess what kind of treatment he had received at Lord Walter's hand.

Jude had somehow hoped Percival would catch one of the hares or squirrels she spotted frequently in the woods, but the falcon persisted in catching only other birds. The birds were tasty but small. Still, Jude wasn't going to complain about the steady stream of warblers, thrushes, and quail Percival brought. She supplemented the nightly catch with gathered berries, nuts, and greens from the forest. She missed the ale and mead that had accompanied most meals at the manor, and the sweets she had always been able to snatch from the kitchen, but at least she wasn't going hungry.

It was almost a shock when she finally reached the outskirts of London. She had not spoken with another human for well over a fortnight, not since she had left Goodwife Middy's small shack. It seemed a lifetime ago. Aware that she was near a village, Jude was careful to build only a small fire, which she put out after eating the sparrow Percival had caught for her. She slept uneasily on the hard ground, tossing from side to side, pulling her cape up on her shoulders even though the night wasn't terribly chilly. As the dawn broke, she gave up on sleep. Feeling tired and confused, she sat on a log, cracking her breakfast of nuts between two stones and composing her thoughts.

Why go to London at all? was the question that kept pressing at her mind. She shook her head violently. She didn't want to admit even to herself that she was frightened of going into the city; she had never in her life been there, and she was afraid of the bandits and thieves she had heard so much about, and of being discovered and sent back home. But she had to get to Kent; that was why she had set out in the first place. She couldn't spend the rest of her life traveling aimlessly through the forest, as appealing as that might be. After all, what would she do when winter came? She would go to London, sell the garnet bracelet, and rest for a day or two. Then she'd find a way to reach Eltham Palace. If there weren't woods in which to hide, if the countryside had towns and villages instead, she would discover a way to travel among people. The rising sun gave her courage, and she remembered Goodwife Middy's assurance that she would reach Kent, that the success of her journey was written in the stars.

That whole day, Jude walked through the country-side surrounding the city, passing large farms and

83

great manor houses. A few people passed her, mostly driving filled wagons drawn by beaten-down work-horses. Again Jude regretted having to send Sheba back into the woods; it would have been painful to sell the horse, but she could have used the money to buy food and a fresh tunic. When she passed a herd of cows, she thought wistfully about fresh butter and milk but knew stopping wasn't a good idea. She pressed on, making good time on the flat dirt road.

Toward midafternoon, she was tired and wished she were back in the enclosed safety of the forest. All around her were open fields and an occasional cottage. The early-summer air was rich with the earthy smell of planting and animals, and she plodded on, dismayed by the problem of finding a bed for the night. Maybe if she passed another manor later on she could find a remote stable in which to sleep. But as the road became increasingly busy, she knew she would have to find an inn. She had only a few coins in her pocket and hated to spend them on a bed. But if she must, she must. No use brooding about it.

As evening fell Jude kept her eye open for a tavern or inn. When she spotted a cottage with a large bunch of ivy over the door, she knew she'd at least find ale and food inside, if not a room. She ripped a length of cloth from the hem of her tunic and wrapped it around the falcon's eyes. "Sorry, Percival," she whispered. "There'll be other people in there, and I don't want you to be uneasy." Then she pushed open the heavy wooden door and walked in.

The room, illuminated only by a pair of candles, was darker than the starlit night. Jude stood just inside the door for a moment until her eyes adjusted to the dimness, then took a good look around. Not a very promising sight. A busty woman in a tight kirtle pumped ale for a few rough-looking men seated at a wooden table. The room had no decorations on the walls, the only spots of color coming from ragged red curtains hanging by the window and the blue apron the barmaid wore, which was none too clean, Jude could tell, even in the dim light. Summoning her courage, she took a seat at the end of the bench, as far away from the others as possible. She laid her sack on the floor and willed Percival to keep quiet from his perch on her shoulder. Now that she'd entered, she couldn't just leave. And there was no telling how far the next tavern might be.

The woman looked up at Jude and gave a smirk. "Can I help you, son?" she asked with less of a country accent than Jude had expected. "We don't see many lads in here. Only randy old goats such as these," and she pointed to the men next to Jude. The men, obviously well into their drinks, laughed loudly. The largest one reached across the table and smacked the woman on her bottom. She raised the cup she was filling as if to splash him with ale, giving a warning:

"That's enough, Smithy, or I'll be calling my man on you."

When they'd settled down a bit, Jude ventured to ask for a cup of ale and some supper. The barmaid poured the ale and told her, "We've only got pease porridge left, lad. We serve our meat in the middle of the day."

"Pease porridge, then." Jude took a long sip of ale. On her empty stomach, she felt the drink relaxing her, making her less wary. When her plate came, she devoured the simple country dish of peas mashed with salt and pepper. She could easily have eaten another whole plate of it but decided not to order more. The penny it had cost was already too dear.

The big man—Smithy—finished the dregs of his drink and turned to question Jude. "What're you doing round these here parts, lad?"

Jude took another swig of ale to fortify herself. She tried to make her voice as deep as possible when she answered. "Heading to London, sir. I'm to be an apprentice musician."

"A musical lad, eh?" Smithy studied the boy. What he saw was a poorly filled-out thing, all skin and bones, with the delicate hands of a girl, who'd probably never done a day's real work in his life. Smithy laid his huge, battered hands on the table and moved his gaze to the falcon. A beautiful peregrine, it was—that would make some prize. Though if *he* had a pet like that, the bird would wear a proper leather hood, not a dirty old strip of cloth. "Who'll you be apprenticed with, boy? I know most round town."

Jude tried not to panic. She didn't like the way this big man was looking at her and at Percival. Her mind racing, she realized that she did know someone in London. "I don't know the Master's name," she said as casually as she could, "for my father arranged it directly with Lionel, the Earl of Wessex. We have ties with his lady, Gwynna."

Smithy eyed the young thing again. In those mud-stained clothes, he didn't look as if he'd have ties with anyone at a manor except the stable boy. But if the lad truly did have connections like that, Smithy wouldn't dare just rough him up and take the falcon. He'd have to be more subtle about it. "It's another half day's journey to the earl's manor. Where will you spend the night?"

Jude gave a shrug, not wanting to talk with this rough man about anything at all, let alone where she'd be sleeping. "Oh, I always find a place. No need to worry about me."

Marian, the barmaid, took pity on the poor young thing. She was a kindhearted woman, one who also knew that Christian charity was often rewarded with more worldly compensation. And those clothes had once been of good quality, though ripped and filthy right now, and that falcon was definitely purebred.

"We've a room upstairs, lad," she told Jude. "Nothing fancy, nothing fitting for the kinsman of an earl, but a room just the same. I'll give it to you for sixpence, but you'll have to pay extra for a meal in the morning."

Smithy slapped the boy's back, hard. He felt Jude wince under the friendly blow and thought again what a scrawny child this was. "It's a good offer, son. You won't find a better one for miles around. Beats sleeping in a barn. Never know what rogues may be around. Better to have a sound roof over your head."

Jude thoroughly regretted ever having set foot in this place. She felt waves of ill will coming from this huge man, and Percival was rocking back and forth on her shoulder in a most disconcerting way, as if he too was uneasy. What could she say? That she was planning on traveling all night? No, he'd know she was lying; the city gates were closed at sundown. That she had friends to stay with? Then he'd ask who, and why she hadn't gone straight there, neither of which questions she could answer. Stifling an agitated sigh, Jude finally answered Marian. "Many thanks, miss. I'll take the room on one condition—breakfast included with the shilling." As a young child, Jude had listened to enough peasants haggling with her father about their rent payments to know she'd be thought a sure fool if she didn't bargain a little.

"Aye, since I like your face, lad, 'tis a deal." Marian

smiled and topped off the boy's glass of ale to seal the bargain.

Jude handed sixpence to the barmaid and drained her cup, hoping to gain some courage from the strong dregs. She decided to sit there until the men had left. If she didn't feel safe in the room, she could always sneak out of the tavern in the night and find some other shelter. She was woefully tired, though. When Marian announced that it was closing time, Jude wiped her mouth on her sleeve and stood, picking up her sack.

" 'Night, lad. Sleep well," Smithy said jovially, slapping Jude on the back again. Jude was sure she'd be all bruises the next day.

" 'Night," she replied blandly, watching the men leave. *Hallelujah, Christ be praised,* she thought as Marian bolted the heavy door behind them. Marian gestured for Jude to follow her up a set of very dark and narrow stairs.

"All done, love?" a voice called from the top of the stairs. There was a muffled hiccup, a loud thump, and then some creative swearing.

"Not quite, Barnabas. We've got a lodger for the night," Marian called back. The upstairs was even darker than below; Marian's candle illuminated only a few feet in front of them. Suddenly a man appeared in the gloom. He was tall and skinny, with dark hair standing out from his head at all angles, and very hairy legs. He wore a rumpled homespun tunic and nothing else, and clutched an empty wineskin in one hand.

"Oh. Greetings to you, young friend." The man nodded in Jude's direction, coming face-to-face with Percival. Barnabas gave a little shriek and jumped back, swearing again.

Marian laughed, more good-naturedly than Jude would have under the same circumstances. "Off to bed with you, Barnabas love. I'll just see this lad to his room, then I'll come join you."

"Bring another wineskin," Barnabas told her sulkily. "And some rags. I seem to have spilled a mite of wine." He turned and disappeared into the darkness.

Marian sighed. "Some strong man to take care of me," she muttered. "Thought I'd not have to work again." She then seemed to remember Jude standing by her side. She opened a door and led Jude in, placing the candlestick on a small table just inside the door. Besides the table, there was a bed—that was all. An empty basin lay on the table, too. Noticing Jude's glance, Marian said, "There's water outside at the pump, if you're interested in washing up. I would have filled the bowl if I'd known earlier that you were staying. Do you need anything else?"

Wordlessly Jude shook her head. Marian said good night and slipped out the door, shutting it softly behind her. Jude sat on the bed, placing her pack in the sliver of space available on the floor. The armoire where she'd put her dresses at home had been at least twice the size of this chamber. Marian had not been joking when she said the room wasn't anything fit for the earl's kinsman.

Jude took Percival off her shoulder, bringing him down to one of the bedposts, where he perched obediently. *What next?* Jude thought. *Should I sleep? Should I climb out the window?* She parted the shabby curtains and looked out. It was a steep drop, no tree branches to grab on the way down. *Well, if I can't get out, no one should be able to get in.* Still in her clothes, Jude lay on the narrow bed and tossed restlessly. Now that her time in the forest was over, it seemed to her like her own golden age—like the Garden of Eden before the Fall. But Jude, religious training steeped into her bones, knew that the Fall of Adam and Eve had been necessary. How else could Redemption come? London might be her fall, she knew; she could only pray that the redemption of the King's Minstrels would follow. Sleep did not come soon, but when it finally did, she dreamed of the forest.

A muffled man's voice woke Jude. She sat bolt upright, disoriented. *Where am I?* She had spent so many nights out in the open that she panicked for a moment when she looked up and saw wood beams instead of a

91

moonlit sky. Percival gave a soft caw, peering at her in the darkness with one yellow eye. "I'm at the tavern," Jude breathed, as much to herself as to Percival. She reached out and stroked his feathers. She took comfort from the warm falcon and did not feel as alone and vulnerable.

Jude leaned over and parted the fabric at the window ever so slightly. By the moonlight she could make out two figures below—Smithy, to be sure, by the large bulk, and one of the others who had been drinking downstairs. They seemed to be having a difficult time of it, trying to get up to the second story of the little house. She watched as Smithy finally hoisted the smaller man onto his back, then to his shoulders.

"Now reach up, Gerd, you addlebrained fool!" Smithy said through his teeth. *Gerd must be heavier than he looked,* Jude thought as she watched Smithy stumble under the weight. He tightened his hold on the rough stones of the tavern's exterior and cursed softly as Gerd kicked him.

"I can't reach!" Gerd whispered, straining his fingertips up to Jude's windowsill. He shifted on Smithy's beefy shoulders and strained upward once again, managing to grab hold of the edge of the windowsill. He hung there, exhausted already, and prepared to haul himself over the sill and through the window.

Jude trembled as she watched the man's slight figure

appear, a dark silhouette against the skimpy curtains. She willed herself to stay calm, getting onto her feet and grabbing the heavy iron basin from the table. As Gerd's foot felt for the floor inside her room, she lunged at him.

But Percival struck first, with a shrill cry and the fervor of a knight in battle. Gerd jumped back, banging his head against the eaves of the low room, stumbling against the window. Percival swirled around him, and he held his hand in front of his face, trying to protect his eyes from the falcon's sharp talons and beak. Jude sprang up on the bed, took aim, and brought the basin crashing down on his head. Gerd gave a little cry and slumped to the floor. With great effort, Jude hauled him up, onto the sill, and out the window. He toppled to the ground, landing directly on Smithy, who had been standing below, waiting for bags of coins and a bound falcon to drop into his waiting arms. Knocked flat by the goatherd, Smithy lay on the ground cursing his luck, the stupid Gerd, and mostly the musician boy. He rubbed his sore head and poked Gerd viciously. "Get up, you knotty-pated simpkin! You mucked up again!"

Jude watched as the two men stumbled up, arguing, not even bothering to keep their voices low, and made their way over the hill to the nearby farmhouses. She sighed and leaned her head against the wooden window frame, stroking Percival and murmuring words of thanks. Then she sat on the little bed, pulled out her pipes, and silently began to practice fingering for a new song she was writing. Only an hour or so until sunrise, and she wasn't taking any more chances on sleeping.

VII

THE ROAD TO LONDON

*J*ude let herself out of the tavern at first light. She felt like a thief, swiping bread and cheese out of the larder and leaving without saying farewell, but breakfast had been agreed upon as part of the room's price. Anyway, she wanted to be on the road before she had the chance to meet with any further mishap. Percival's makeshift hood was wrapped around his eyes, for she did not want him to stray far from her, swooping after prey. She hurried along the dirt road, wishing again for the forest's cover. Around her, farmers were harnessing horses and oxen, serfs were beginning their long day of tilling and hoeing. As the sun finally came up full force over the eastern horizon, Jude relaxed a little, slowed down, and munched on her breakfast. She should be in London by midday. Maybe she could find a tavern that sold meat pies or mutton stew. She chewed the bread and cheese, but her stomach, unsatisfied, was ready for heartier fare.

She was rounding a sharp turn in the road, passing by a large stone well that looked as if it had been dry for many a year, when Smithy jumped her. Springing out from behind the well, he landed on Jude full force, sending her sprawling to the ground and knocking the breath out of her chest with his weight.

Jude screamed, a furious, bloodcurdling sound, and desperately tried to reach her belt knife. But the man smacked her hard across the face, whipping her head back. "Shut yer trap, you young ragpicker." Holding both her arms tight over her head with one beefy hand, he fumbled in her belt pouch with the other.

Percival, who had been knocked clear off Jude's shoulder and had managed to dislodge his hood, circled around his mistress's attacker twice before diving at Smithy, talons wide open and screaming with rage. He landed right on the man's back, digging in and going for the neck, as if after another bird of prey.

It was Smithy's turn to scream as the talons raked his skin and the bird's sharp beak drew blood. Smithy released Jude's arms and turned on Percival, grabbing the falcon's neck, wrenching the bird off him, and hurling him far into the next field.

Jude had her knife ready when Smithy's attention returned to her. Concern for Percival flashed through her mind, but she had only a second's thought for the falcon. She knew that Smithy could kill her with a couple of hard blows and throw her down the well. She wouldn't be found for weeks, and there would be no way for anyone to identify her body. Chasing that grim thought from her mind, she concentrated on the situation at hand.

Blood was pouring from Smithy's neck and back when he turned again to Jude. "Damn you to Hell!" he cried. His fury increasing, he grabbed Jude's right hand and snapped the knife out of it, then gave her a violent clout on the head. Jude stumbled and sank to her knees, reeling. Smithy followed with another blow, knocking her out cold. Bleeding and cursing, he went through Jude's meager possessions, swearing even more as he discovered how few coins the lad had. The garnet bracelet would fetch a decent price, and the breeches were good quality, though well worn, but there were no pouches full of gold. He flung Jude's pipe onto the ground, along with the sachets of powder given to her by Goodwife Middy. The rest he gathered up into a bundle and tucked into his own sack. He was debating whether to throw the boy in the well or slit his throat and *then* throw him in the well, when he heard the clatter of wheels and the muffled *clop-clop* of horses' hooves. Staggering a little, Smithy gathered up his plunder and hurried in the opposite direction from the approaching wagon.

When William Langley, chief tenant farmer of Waltham, rounded the corner by the old well and saw Jude's body, he exclaimed, "God's bones! Not another dead boy!" With a single quick pull on the reins he stopped his four strong spotted horses from their energetic trot and reluctantly climbed down from the wagon. He'd gotten a late start already, what with those lazy peasants taking their time loading the vegetables and meats, and then Jewel, his prize mare, needing to be reshod and that stupid fat blacksmith nowhere to be found. They'd had to send to the next town for a smith to replace Jewel's left rear shoe, and the sun had been well into the sky before he'd been able to set out. And now this.

He sighed. The earl hated to hear about the deaths of these young boys, heading to London for apprenticeships or to make their fortunes in other ways. The bandits on this road were a menace, and more than one lad had turned up dead in that damned dry well. It would be well past midmorning by the time Langley got to London, to present the summer's first crops and meats to the earl and the bishop. Langley always hated this time of year—time to present his rent and tithe. He was a God-fearing and King-loving man, yes, he was, but having to share the products of his backbreaking labor with those who already had so much . . . well, it never struck him as quite fair. It wasn't as if the bishop would go hungry for want of his food, nor the good Earl of Wessex, neither. And Langley had seven hungry mouths to feed at home, and another on its way, and a lawsuit pending by his covetous neighbor, who claimed Langley's most fertile field as his own. The farmer was feeling decidedly uncharitable when he bent over the unconscious Jude.

Langley held his hand below Jude's nostrils and felt the faint breath. "Well, he's alive, glory be," he muttered. He crouched, undecided for a moment, then scooped Jude up and placed the limp body in the full wagon, wedging it between a side of beef and a large sack of onions. He tossed Jude's nearly empty pack in after, with the few items that lay on the road. Better to bring the young fellow into London and dump him on some physician there, Langley decided. Too many people at home already, and the early morning half gone. He flicked the reins, said, "Giddy up," and the horses broke into a trot once again. Langley, still muttering to himself about the unfairness of tithe and rent, failed to notice a peregrine falcon, dirt and blood obscuring its handsome patterns, which flew crookedly out of the adjoining field and settled in the back of the wagon, next to the injured youth.

Jude was first conscious of her head. The pounding felt as if she were being thrashed over and over again with a heavy flail. Then she felt movement, the rocking back and forth, the not-so-gentle bumping. And soon she became aware of the rest of her body, wedged tight between something hard and smelly on one side and something lumpy and smelly on the other. The heat beat down on her, and as she opened her eyes to the glaring sun, she separated her parched lips and stuck out her tongue. Her mouth felt as dry and dusty as clay. She shook her head, trying to clear the deep fog within, trying to remember where she was and what had brought her here. She sat up cautiously, holding her aching head. *By Mary! Where am I?*

Inching up ever so slowly, she discovered the side of beef and the bag of onions that had been making her rest so uncomfortable. "I'm in a wagon," she whispered, barely able to get the words out because she was so thirsty. The fight with Smithy came back to her all in a rush, and she groaned, not from her injuries but from the memory.

As if he understood, Percival poked his head up from the cool bushel of leeks where he'd been hiding to keep out of the sun. He gave a short caw and nudged Jude with his head. Jude gathered the falcon to her chest, giving a silent prayer of thanks that they were both still alive. Percival looked half dead, the poor bird, but she'd find a way to fix him up. Right now she needed something to drink, and fast, before she lost consciousness again.

Cautiously moving her bruised and battered limbs, she edged her way up to the front of the moving wagon. "Sir," she croaked, trying to get the attention of the man driving. She shot an admiring glance at the team of horses, then looked again at the man. He was dressed like a farmer, but his clothes were fresh and his boots handsome and well shaped. He was muttering to himself.

"Sir!" Jude felt as if she were shouting, but the word came out as a low gasp. Nevertheless, Langley heard and gave a start, then turned to see the lad crouching in the wagon, on top of a large wheel of cheese. The boy's face was bright red, and the blood spots on his tunic had dried to a muddy brown. He looked a sight, for sure. He pointed beseechingly at Langley's flask, moving his mouth as if to speak, but no words came out. Grudgingly the farmer handed over the skin of ale and watched out of the corner of his eye as the bedraggled youth guzzled down near half of the contents. When Jude's thirst was finally sated, she handed back the flask with a grateful, "Thankee, sir. I was parched. May I ask where we be?" She adopted the local manner of speech as best she could.

"Near London, if you need be told," Langley replied grumpily. "You were half dead in Waltham, so I piled you in the back and thought to find a physician in the city. Always thieves and bandits on that road."

"Aye, and I seem to be a bit worse for wear from the attentions of one." Jude tried to brush the caked blood off her tunic, to no avail. At least it wasn't her own blood, she reasoned. Percival hopped out from the leek bushel and landed on her shoulder.

"That your bird?" Langley asked with surprise. A peregrine, even in the poor state this one was in, was a gentleman's pet.

"Aye. I think he was what the bandit wanted. But Percival had other plans." She stroked his feathers gently.

"Percival, eh?" If this lad was a gentleman's son, there might be some reward for having taken him up. After all the boy probably would have died, lying there in the road. "You want to come over here and ride on the seat, where there's less jostle?"

With great care, Jude climbed over the side of the wagon and stepped onto the seat, Langley having moved to one side to make room. With Percival on her shoulder, Jude settled in comfortably, thankful to be out of the back. Langley handed her the skin again and she took another grateful gulp. "And may I ask what day this might be?"

Langley raised his eyebrows. The beating must have addled the boy's brains, if he could not remember the day. " 'Tis the second day after the Feast of St. Thomas—the fifth day of July. The fourth year of King Edward the Third," he added for good measure. "So, I suppose you were headed to London, lad. Your father sent you, eh? For an apprenticeship?" The farmer wanted details about the boy's family. Maybe he was going to stay with wealthy relatives.

"Aye, I was heading toward London." Jude's thoughts tumbled over each other as she tried to think up a proper tale. She had told the story already of going to visit Lionel; maybe she should stick with that. *I'd love to see Gwynna,* she thought, with a deep pang of what felt like homesickness. It had been a long time since she'd spoken with a friend.

That decided it. Dropping the local dialect, Jude continued, "I'm on my way south to Kent, truth be told, but must first pay a visit to the Earl of Wessex. I have ties with his lady, Gwynna."

Langley stared and could hardly suppress a grin. "But the earl is the lord of our fief!" he cried. He was delighted—at least the boy who had made footprints on that prize cheese was kin to his lord's lady. "I'm heading to his manor today, with the rent payment for our land." He gestured behind him, to the food in the wagon. "Also to the bishop, with our tithe," he added with less pleasure.

"You're bound for the manor now?"

"Aye. Should be there shortly after dinner." Langley had hoped to get there in time for the midday meal, but all the delays made that impossible.

Jude stared at the passing scene, relieved not to be walking through the outlying districts of town, with their squalid little houses and disreputable-looking inhabitants. She couldn't believe her luck. Gwynna would take care of her, just as she'd done at the convent all those years ago. She closed her eyes, preparing already for the happy reunion.

Then her eyes flew open. She was supposed to be a boy. Gwynna would know her, of course, but her husband must never learn the truth. Even if Lionel understood her plight and wished to help her, he would be compelled, by law and obligation, to send her home if he found out that she was a girl who had run away. Jude had been outside the law since she had left her stepfather's manor without the protection of a husband. As they rode closer and closer to London, Jude wracked her already muddled brain to discover a way of alerting Gwynna not to expose her secret.

VIII

LONDON TOWNE

*I*n spite of the circumstances that had brought her to Langley's cart, Jude was thankful for a guide to take her past the outskirts of town and through the gates into the imposing walled city of London. She would have been hard-pressed to find Lionel's manor on her own, even though its squadron of symmetrical towers dominated the surrounding landscape. She had never before seen so many buildings. She stared, open-mouthed, as they drove through town, while all the noise made her head spin: the children's and peddlers' cries, the crashing of iron wagon wheels on stone, the hourly chiming of bells from more than a hundred churches. This was a different world entirely from the villages of her father's manor and her convent school.

Here the cottages stood practically side by side, with

gardens no bigger than one of her mother's shawls. There were few animals in the gardens, but more people than Jude thought she had ever seen in her whole life—and they were all there, at once! Merchants with loaded carts rumbled along the narrow streets, while others peddled their wares from small stalls or from large sacks hung on their backs; women pumped water from the central well, or knelt in their tiny gardens over great washtubs, or sat spinning in their cottages with the wooden doors and shutters open, letting in the midday sun; and everywhere children ran afoot, carrying buckets of water, or piles of laundry, or younger siblings too small to walk on their own.

The dirt road abruptly changed to a cobblestone one, and they bumped along more slowly, passing larger cottages, then houses with grander stretches of land, and finally coming to an enormous manor on top of a hill, surrounded by a stone wall and guarded by more than a dozen soldiers. Flags flew from the two highest towers.

Jude craned her neck to see the lofty towers that topped the manor, and then they were riding through the huge doors of the gatehouse, which now stood open.

"Is this Windsor Castle?" she whispered, her voice trembling.

Langley laughed out loud, comfortable in his exalted position of bringing supplies to the earl. He remembered his own anxiety and awe on his first visit—nay, also on his second and third—and felt puffed up by this lad's obvious wonder and fear. "Nay, my boy, 'tis but the earl's. I've never been to the royal castle myself, but have heard that 'tis many, many times bigger than this, and that more than one hundred guards stand posted every hour of the day and night."

The cart finally came to a halt in an inner courtyard, with the main doors looming ahead of them. A groom appeared, unharnessed the four tired horses, and led them off to the stables to be curried, fed, and watered; then several people from the kitchens approached: the clerk of the kitchen, yeomen of the pantry and cellar, and three pantry servants. Greeting Langley familiarly, the servants began to unload the cart, while the clerk solemnly recorded each item in a large leather book, and the yeomen gave precise orders as to where each bushel or barrel should go.

As the cart was unloaded, Langley pointed out the special merit of each piece to the yeomen and the clerk, telling with what care this cheese was prepared, what fine grain that was. He seemed to forget entirely about Jude, who sat on the wagon for a while, trying to collect her wits. Eventually, however, she climbed down and joined Langley, although she felt self-conscious about her torn and bloody tunic and the cuts and scratches on her face. Langley and the servants all were neat and clean, and the clerk and yeomen, who were gentlemen, looked at her as if she were some beggar who had wandered in from the square.

Noticing the clerk's withering look, Langley remembered his traveling companion and his hopes to gain favor with the earl. "This lad has ties to Lady Gwynna," he announced suddenly, and the clerk raised his eyes in disbelief.

" 'Tis true, sir," Jude assured him in her most proper voice, with a slight bow. "I was beset by a bandit on the road to London, and this kind farmer assisted me and brought me here. If I may but write a note to the earl and his lady, I am sure that they will see me."

The clerk had been planning to refuse this bedraggled stranger's request, but he was well-spoken and claimed to know how to write. And that falcon on his shoulder, although grimy and matted, certainly had a peregrine's markings under the dirt and blood. The clerk wondered how the bird had escaped from a bandit, but instead of asking, handed the lad a scrap of parchment and a charcoal stick to write with. It was not his place to question visitors of the earl.

Jude, who by now had formed her plan, scratched the note quickly and handed it back to the clerk with a silent prayer. The clerk in turn handed it to the gentleman usher, who read it and handed it to a messenger, who ran with it to the great hall, where Lionel and Gwynna had already finished their dinner. They had had few guests, only five-and-twenty or so, along with the various clerics, aldermen, auditors, and other town officials who had business at the manor, so it had been an intimate dinner, and they had been well entertained by a traveling band of players. When the messenger appeared the guests were just beginning to push back their benches and go their separate ways, reluctantly returning to everyday tasks.

Gwynna, who was always glad when dinner was over and all those dreary guests left, took the piece of parchment warily. An unexpected note could mean the sudden arrival of a relative or some other acquaintance of noble birth, and it was not unusual for a guest to visit with more than a hundred members of his household, as they traveled from one residence to another. Lionel's cousin, the Earl of Salisbury, typically waited until later in the summer to move his household to his Norwich home; as she opened the note, Gwynna sent a quick prayer to the Virgin that her peace would not be shattered so soon by Salisbury's rowdy entourage.

The note, however, had no distinctive seal on it, and she read it through twice, then a third time, before she fully understood. She finally handed it to her husband, both smiling and shaking her head in disbelief.

The note said:

Right worthy and worshipful Lord and Lady,

I greet you well, and commend myself to you. We have not yet made acquaintance, but I have heard much about you from my sister Judith. I am Stephen of Nesscliff, younger son of Lord Walter and Lady Cecilia. I have recently come to London, and would like to pay my compliments to the dear friends of my sister.

Written in London at the castle gates, this V day of July.

Jude shook so slightly that no one noticed her trembling, but she was painfully aware of her heart's pounding as she was introduced to the earl. At least they had fed her first, and a physician had washed and dressed the wound on her head and bathed the large bruise on her left cheek with healing water. The falconer had coaxed Percival away to the mews to take care of his scratches and injuries. A yeoman of the wardrobe had found a clean tunic and pair of breeches, but Jude dismissed him from the chamber before she undressed, washed off the blood that was spattered over her, and put on the clean clothes. The yeoman was rather insulted at this dismissal, being used to fulfilling his obligation to attend the earl's male visitors of high rank, but he had the good training not to mention the slight to his master.

"Stephen, Stephen, Stephen," Jude muttered under her breath as she laced up her boots. She repeated the name to herself over and over as a young squire called for her and led her to the main hall. He held the door for her, and she entered a large, ornate room with double windows and dark tapestries lining the walls. A richly colored coat of arms hung prominently over the chimneypiece, announcing to all visitors Lionel's kinship with the King. At the far end of the room, a lord and a lady, both impressively dressed and looking much older than Jude, sat poring over a large book.

For a moment Jude almost panicked, thinking the squire had brought her to the wrong chamber, but then the lady stood and held out her arms. Jude saw the flaming red hair and the merry green eyes and knew it was her dear friend. She crossed the room with large strides and grasped Gwynna's hands in her own, stopping herself only at the last minute from throwing herself into her friend's arms. Squeezing Gwynna's hands, she chastised herself—Stephen would not have embraced this lady. She knew she should speak, but her voice stuck in her throat, and the words of greeting remained unspoken.

Gwynna recovered first "I greet you with God's blessing. 'Tis such an honor to meet you, Lord Stephen," she choked out, her voice strange with emotion, confusion, and hidden laughter. "I heard much of you from your sister, in the convent. How is dear Lady Judith?"

Jude drew a deep, ragged breath. "She is betrothed to the Baron Caerleon. She is resigned to marry him and be a mother to his five daughters." Their eyes met, and then Gwynna understood. She gave Jude's hands a final squeeze and dropped them, turning to her husband.

She made the brief introduction: "My lord, may I present Stephen of Nesscliff? My husband, Lionel," and the two bowed to each other. Jude was relieved to see what a handsome man the earl was, with sparkling eyes and a smile that came easily to his lips.

"Welcome, Lord Stephen. My gentleman usher told me of your misfortune at the hands of a bandit. I trust that my servants have taken care of your needs," he said, waving to Jude to be seated.

"Aye, my lord. Your physician has treated my wounds and given me healing water and herbs." Jude touched the bandage on her head and winced at the contact. Gwynna made a sympathetic noise, but Jude continued. "And I was so generously given food and clean clothing to wear. I thank you for your hospitality, my lord. I must also commend your tenant farmer Langley, who put me in his wagon while I still lay insensible and provided me with transport here."

"He shall be rewarded for his beneficence." Lionel rang a small bell and gave quick instructions to the servant who appeared: William Langley, chief tenant farmer of Waltham, would be bestowed with an extra field of fertile land as a special grant from the earl. Jude leaned back in relief, feeling certain that not only was her debt now repaid, but that forever after Langley would pick up any "dead boys" he found by the well.

Business attended to, Lionel turned back to his guest. "From my wife's stories, you are an exact copy of your sister. How many years younger are you than she?"

"Two, my lord. I was just eleven years in the spring."

"And tall for your age, like your sister." Lionel took in the fair hair and attractive features. This Stephen was a mite young for his sister Christina, but the girl was already fifteen and had refused legions of other suitors. Last year, when he had begun negotiations for her marriage to Richard, Earl of Colchester, they had come to nothing. Colchester had made no more communications after he had actually met Christina. Lionel thought with a mental sigh of how difficult his sister had been since their parents died, and how he was constantly failing in his one duty regarding her— to have her married off safely Lionel would introduce the two and see if she took a fancy to this young lord.

"I'll leave you now; I know how much my lady has wanted to speak with you." He rose and strode toward the door, his mind already turning from Christina to the accounts he needed to go over with his steward and comptroller. At the threshold he stopped and said, "You must play for us at supper. Are you as proficient a musician as your sister, Lord Stephen?"

Jude smiled. "*I* think so, my lord, but Lady Judith believes herself superior."

With a bark of laughter, Lionel left the chamber, thoughtfully shutting the door behind him.

Gwynna carefully closed the heavy cover of her account book of guests. She felt her senses must be deceiving her. Could Judith really have run away? Gwynna herself had never been the most obedient of children—she had broken rules at the convent and plagued her father and mother no end—but she still held some things sacred and inviolable. "Well," she said, after a moment of eyeing Jude from head to toe. "This certainly is a surprise, 'Lord Stephen.' You're fortunate to find us in London now. The household only returned from Bristol a fortnight ago."

"What else could I do?" Jude whispered, ignoring Gwynna's formality. "My stepfather was truly going to marry me to an old man with five daughters. Gwynna, he had a gray beard and made rude remarks and pinched my bottom and picked his teeth with a knife and wiped his mouth on the tablecloth. I *couldn't* marry him. I would have died."

"Hush, now," Gwynna comforted her. " 'Tis not right for a grown boy like you to be crying."

Jude laughed, then flinched from the pain it caused in her cheekbone. " 'Tis hard to keep remembering I'm a lad."

Gwynna's expression was serious. "You must remember. Lionel is not a jealous man, but the pages and gentlewomen watch everything," she whispered. "We must be careful not to be too affectionate, else rumors might be started."

Jude nodded, inching away from Gwynna on the low seat they shared. She hadn't thought of *that* complication of her being a boy. Now Gwynna laughed and took Jude's arm. "Don't be ridiculous—I just meant that you must think before you cry or embrace me. Come, I'll show you about the manor, then we can walk in the garden and you can tell me all of your wild adventures."

IX

CHRISTINA

*L*ionel himself performed the introduction. "Lady Christina, may I present Lord Stephen of Nesscliff." The young lady curtsied low, but kept her eyes on Jude. Jude bowed nervously, a suspicion growing in her mind from the oversolicitous way Lionel was watching them, and also from the way this stunning woman held her eyes. For stunning she was. Christina had pale golden hair, coiled simply on top of her head. She wore a rose-colored gown with gold embroidery at the wrists, and a delicate gold chain circled her slim neck. Christina was easily the most beautiful lady Jude had ever met, more beautiful than Jude's own mother, or Gwynna, or even Gwynna's older sister Sabrene, who had joined them for supper, along with her husband and their accompanying knights and gentlewomen. Jude gulped nervously and stammered her replies as Christina took her arm and led her to table. She really believes I'm a *he,* Jude thought incredulously, and more than a little nervously.

Gwynna had arranged for an intimate supper in the great chamber, rather than in the larger hall: just the family and the most important yeomen and gentlefolk, to welcome "Lord Stephen." She had thought correctly that Judith would be less overwhelmed in acting her role before a small audience, but she hadn't counted on her husband's playing matchmaker. Watching Judith's panicked face as she was seated next to Christina, Gwynna shook her head, and whispered to Lionel, "My dear, Lord Stephen is much too young for Christina. He's but a boy!"

Lionel patted her arm. "But look at how she takes to him!" he whispered back. "Think of how many men she's turned away. If she likes this lad . . ." His voice trailed off as he watched the couple happily.

While the chaplain intoned grace Christina peeked at Lord Stephen out of the corner of her eye. He was young, but at least he was several inches taller than she. And not major nobility—not like herself, with ties to the King—but that was an asset, too. Christina didn't know much about marriage, but she knew that it was a losing battle for a woman. All the glory went to the husband—the title, the land, the revenues collected from the peasants. And the wife had to do all the hard work, bearing the children, entertaining the guests, keeping the household running smoothly. She almost sighed out loud thinking about it.

But Christina had promised herself this: she would not be the inferior of her husband. He might be of the stronger sex, but she would have the advantages of age and rank. So far, the lords who had come to pay suit had all either outranked her, or been much too old. This lad here, though, was perfect in age and rank, and he was a delight to look at, as well, despite the bandage around his head and the angry bruise on his cheek. By the time the priest had finished droning on in Latin, Christina had made up her mind. She would marry young Stephen of Nesscliff. So what if he did not yet have a beard? If they were betrothed this autumn, they could be married in the spring, perhaps on his twelfth birthday.

The yeoman carver made quick work of the roast and then walked around the table, serving. Jude noticed a taster standing behind Lionel, and thought what a dreary job that would be, making sure the lord didn't get poisoned. She was glad the food was accepted by the taster, for then Lionel dug into his meal, the signal for everyone else to start eating, too. The venison was exquisite, in its spicy cream sauce, served next to bright yellow saffron rice with almonds. Jude helped herself to a huge portion of salad, thinking how much she had missed good dressed greens while she was traveling. Christina raised her eyebrows a little at the way Jude ate, but Jude continued to put away a huge amount of food. *I'm a growing boy,* she thought with a smile.

They had eaten the fruit and cheese and were moving on to a sweet custard when Lionel addressed Jude. "So, Lord Stephen, tell us your plans. Shall you be settling in London?"

Jude allowed herself one bite of the creamy custard before she answered. "Nay, my lord, I'm sorry to say that I am only in London for a short while. I am traveling to Kent, to study music and become an apprentice with the King's Minstrels."

There was a long silence after she made this announcement. Trying to ignore the implications, Jude took another bite of dessert. *By Mary,* she thought, *this is the best custard I've ever had.* She licked the spoon thoroughly.

"A minstrel?" Christina asked, confused. *Why in the world would he want to be a minstrel?*

"A musician?" Lionel was slightly distressed by the news. But then he was heartened—Stephen would surely fall in love with Christina, and decide to stay.

"What a wonderful idea!" Gwynna announced. She picked up her spoon and finally dug into the custard, relieved. *Let's get Judith out of here as quickly as possible.*

She loved her friend, but she could see no good ending if Christina decided she wanted "Stephen" to court her.

Lionel and Christina both turned and scowled at Gwynna. Gwynna ignored them and continued to eat. Amazing how much they look alike, she thought calmly, despite their different hair colors. Both such handsome people.

"Music is the thing I'm best at," Jude continued, hoping to get Christina and Lionel to stop frowning. "It's always been that way. My mother and stepfather tried to interest me in fighting, or studies, or even the priesthood, but I had no talent for anything but tuning, playing, singing, and storytelling." Gwynna looked at Judith with admiration. She had been worried about her ability to keep up the façade, but the girl lied like a professional bandit.

Lionel leaned across the table to question Stephen further. "You didn't like jousting?"

"Nay. I enjoy riding, but always dropped my lance when fighting."

"And did your stepfather have you assist with keeping the manor's books, and collecting taxes?"

"Aye, he did. But I'm terrible at sums, and I never made the serfs pay up. I was always too interested in hearing what new songs they sang."

Lionel decided not to ask about the lad's lack of

religious vocation. Stephen's deciding to be a priest would be even worse than his becoming a musician. Being one of the King's Minstrels was much superior to being a typical minstrel, Lionel admitted grudgingly, but his sister could never, never marry a professional musician, even one of the King's. Especially since that required years of training—training that took place nearly a hundred miles away.

Christina, with the confidence of a young woman with beauty, rank, and fortune, thought, *He'll fall in love with me, and then he'll never want to leave.* Aloud, she said, "Come, Lord Stephen. If music is what you enjoy best, let us play." She nodded to the chaplain, who mumbled another long prayer to signal the end of the meal, while Christina tapped her foot impatiently. When grace was finally done, Christina extended her hand. Jude could do nothing but take it and be led to the shelves where various instruments lay. Christina gestured for her guest to pick; after a little thought, Jude chose a beautiful little lute, like the kind Minstrel Robin had played so many weeks ago at her betrothal banquet. The pear-shaped instrument was made of a shiny light wood, and as Jude strummed the strings, the sound it made matched its delicate appearance.

"Do you know the song 'Bonny Barbara Allen'?" Christina asked, laying her hand lightly on Jude's arm. Jude nodded.

"Would you like an instrument? A harp would go nicely." Jude gestured to a lap-harp that sat on the shelf.

Christina laughed her delightful laugh and, shaking her head, replied, "Nay, Lord Stephen. You shy away from jousting and sums, I from playing. But I shall sing." She took a deep breath and waited for her guest to start strumming the tune. She held her head high and smiled, because she knew how beautiful she looked, and what a lovely, pure voice she had. *He'll surely fall in love when he hears me sing,* she thought smugly. *They always do.*

Jude plucked the opening notes and let Christina begin.

> *"It was in and about Martinmas time,*
> *When the green leaves were a-falling,*
> *That Sir John Graeme, in the West Country,*
> *Fell in love with Barbara Allen."*

Jude listened carefully, then joined in for the rest, her low voice harmonizing well with Christina's high one. Not too bad, Jude decided, as they came to the end, Jude strumming the final chords more and more softly, as if to mimic the girl's sorrow.

> *"O mother, mother, make my bed,*
> *O make it soft and narrow,*

Since my love died for me today
I'll die for him tomorrow."

Christina's voice wasn't bad at all; a little high for Jude's taste, and tending a bit much toward fancy additions to the music, when Jude preferred to keep a tune simpler, more spare. But it would suffice for duets.

Christina was elated. She could tell that her singing had done it again, by the way Stephen watched her so closely when she added those extra trills in the song. She could barely hide her triumphant smile as she requested they now sing "Alisoun," another romantic song. *We'll announce our betrothal on Lammas Day, the harvest festival celebrated on the first day of August—that will signify a long and fruitful marriage. And I'll have a wedding gown of velvet,* she thought. *Velvet with taffeta and lace and whatever other expensive and rare materials we can find. Stephen will give me a betrothal ring of sapphires—they so complement my eyes—and a matching necklace, and I will have the most lavish wedding banquet that anyone has seen since the King married. And I think I'll invite all my failed suitors to the feast, to show off my handsome young husband. There will be days of tournaments and jousting following the ceremony, and every lady for miles around will envy me.*

After three more such slow, romantic ballads, Jude was thoroughly bored with her duet companion. Her head wound was starting to throb again, and she was losing patience. She decided she disliked trills and high sopranos, and was going to flee from the great hall if Christina gave her one more of those deep, intimate looks. "Shall we *all* sing?" Jude suggested, as Christina took another deep breath in preparation for their sixth duet. "I know this jolly song about King Arthur . . ."

"Nay, we prefer to hear you two sing," Lionel answered quickly.

Gwynna shot him an annoyed look. "My dear, perhaps you don't care to sing, but I'm sure the rest of us do." She rose, and with her went her sister, Sabrene—smiling, because she was fonder of singing than of listening—and Sabrene's husband, Vincent, Earl of Prestbury. Gwynna also gestured for the steward and the other gentlemen at the head-officers' table to join them. Sabrene took up the harp that Christina had rejected, and Gwynna found some bells to shake. Jude made quick work of teaching the chorus to the group, and they launched into the ballad. Lionel, though irritated that Stephen had not wanted to continue singing alone with Christina, had to admit that the lad sounded quite the professional, the way he fingered that lute, and got everyone joining in for the chorus. He'd make a fine member of the King's Minstrels. But Lionel spared little thought for the pleasure of King Edward. This young Stephen was going to stay and marry Lady Christina. Lionel's mind was made up.

X

TO MARKET

"Where have you been?" Gwynna demanded, out of breath from searching what seemed like the entire manor and grounds and out of sorts from having to fend off her gentlewomen attendants, all of whom wanted to walk with her on this beautiful summer day.

"Why, here, of course," Jude answered pleasantly. After early Mass in the family gallery of the chapel, she'd come to the mews for a lovely morning of preening Percival's feathers and laughing while he amused himself with the other falcons. She'd taken him out to the courtyard for a flight and had been delighted with the way the bird had recovered from his wounds. Jude's own injuries were well healed now, and her largest bruise faded to yellow. It was already late July, four days past the Feast of St. James the Greater, and Jude was growing more and more comfortable at the luxurious manor.

"Well, I've been looking all over for you." Gwynna huffed for another moment, then changed tone. "Lord Stephen, I had especially wanted to show you the orchards," she said in a honeyed voice.

Jude looked up from Percival, surprised. "But I've seen the orchards already." Then she noticed Gwynna's quick blink in the direction of Benedict, the old falconer. "Oh, you mean the *orchards,*" Jude continued, cursing her own stupidity. They surely couldn't talk in front of the falconer. Jude shook her head as she placed Percival on the new leather padding she'd wrapped around her forearm. It was so peculiar—Jude was going longer and longer stretches before she remembered that she wasn't really Lord Stephen, that she was just playing a role. She nodded her thanks to Benedict, then the two friends strolled out to the apple and cherry orchards, walking the paved avenues between the flowering trees.

When they were out of earshot of the various gardeners working on the grounds, Gwynna announced to Jude, "My husband and his sister are preparing your wedding. To Christina." She expected shocked cries from Jude, but instead her friend just smiled.

"Yes, I thought as much."

Gwynna sighed, exasperated. "And what are you going to do? Marry her?" she asked sarcastically.

"Why do I have to do anything? She'll soon see that I don't love her, and that I really do plan on traveling to Kent to be an apprentice. Why should it be a problem? A lady as beautiful as she shouldn't have any difficulty finding a husband."

"No, but you don't understand Christina. She wants *you*. Perhaps because you're the only eligible man around who hasn't fallen down at the sight of her and kissed her feet," Gwynna replied with scorn.

"But I'm not a man and I'm not eligible. Are you saying I must leave now, Gwynna? Is that what you want?"

Gwynna stopped walking and faced her friend. "Nay, Judith, I want you to stay. I simply don't know how long we can keep up this deceit if Christina believes herself in love with you."

"I can manage her, don't you worry." Jude patted Gwynna's hand, and they continued walking. "As a last resort, I can tell her that my heart belongs to another."

Gwynna shook her head. "That will only make you more desirable, Jude. Maybe you should pretend to love her instead, and she will then turn from you, as she has from all her other suitors."

Jude smiled, but said nothing. Gwynna watched her,

drinking in the sight of this seemingly unperturbed young man, handsome and confident, with a regal falcon on his arm. "You've changed, Judith, from the young girl who cried silent tears in bed because a grouchy old nun called her wicked."

At that Jude laughed and turned merry eyes to Gwynna. "You're my dearest, oldest friend," she said, and her eyes did fill with tears. "And I would embrace you, but the servants would talk!"

Now Gwynna laughed and squeezed Jude's arm. They came to the last row of trees and then turned around, walking back to the manor.

Christina was waiting for them when they returned, seated on a wooden bench within the main courtyard, working on a tiny piece of embroidery. From this bench she could see for what seemed like miles in three directions and would know where anyone walked who was touring the gardens, orchards, stables, dovecotes, or beehives. It was her favorite spot. As soon as she saw the figures approaching, she ordered her attending gentlewoman to leave her alone. She wished Gwynna, too, could be sent away with a single word.

"Lord Stephen, Lady Gwynna!" Christina exclaimed in a surprised tone of voice. She rose from the bench and curtseyed low, giving Lord Stephen a perfect view of her white throat and lovely bosom. "How unexpected to see you here." She had only been waiting an hour for Stephen to return from the mews.

"Lady Christina," Jude and Gwynna murmured in return, bowing and curtseying to the young woman.

"Lionel tells me there's to be a market in town tomorrow, with merchants from many faraway lands," Christina told them, seated once again with her needlework in hand.

Jude stared at the embroidery. Like everything else about Christina, it looked perfect, with stitches so tiny Jude could hardly tell where one ended and another began. It was a pattern of minute flowers surrounded by a gold border; the background had flecks of silver. Jude had never seen gold or silver thread before, and she was overcome—not for the first time—with two opposite feelings: how lucky Christina was, to be so beautiful and have so many material goods at her disposal, and how lucky she herself was to have escaped from a life of embroidery, and of needing to marry simply because she was female.

Christina continued in her calm voice, "I was desperately hoping to find a silk merchant." She didn't sound desperate at all; in fact, she smiled up at Jude while she spoke. "But my brother insists that he is too busy to come to town with me, since the new abbot will be visiting to discuss business." Christina stuck her lower lip out just slightly, producing what she knew was a very attractive pout. "And he said that I mustn't go alone, that it's too dangerous." She sighed, and focused her eyes on the embroidery again, but she waited expectantly for Stephen's offer.

It came, of course. "Why, I can take you," Jude told her, smiling at the thought of *her* protecting anyone. "And Lady Gwynna, as well. We should have a lovely time, and then Lady Christina can buy all the silk she needs."

Both Christina and Gwynna scowled at Jude; Christina, because she wanted to be alone with Stephen, and Gwynna, because she did not want Jude spending any time at all with Christina. *But it's too late,* Gwynna thought. She just hoped that Lionel wouldn't be terribly angry at her if he ever discovered this deception. Christina's mind raced, busy searching for a way to get Gwynna to remain at the manor. Nothing occurred to her at the moment, but she knew she'd think of a plan.

"Oh, Gwynna, I'm so dreadfully sorry you can't come with us," Christina purred as she fastened her light cloak around her neck with a narrow silk cord. The cloak was to help keep the city's dust and dirt off her dress; as it was the end of the summer, she did not need it for warmth. "It's such a shame that Lionel decided he needed your help in greeting the new abbot." Christina hoped she sounded sincere; in fact, it had been she who had whispered to her brother last night that the abbot might feel slighted if the lady of the castle weren't there.

Gwynna gave a humorless smile and wished them a good time. "Be careful," she warned Jude. "There are a lot of dangers in the city." The real danger, she knew, was that Christina would provoke Jude into telling the truth. As for other perils . . . well, she almost wished that some Arabian trader would kidnap her sister-in-law. Gwynna knew who had put the idea into Lionel's head that she should stay, and she truly had been looking forward to the market. Especially since the abbot was going to be Lionel's guest for the evening meal, it had seemed that she would have ample time to meet him; but her husband had insisted she remain at home, and so she obeyed. Gwynna's high-spirited disobedience as a child had often been overlooked at the convent and manor house; willfulness with her husband, however, would have been unseemly, and Gwynna rarely chose to challenge him.

A groom helped Christina position herself and her voluminous skirts on her beautiful white mare, while Jude mounted a dappled gray. Percival, completely mended and his torn feathers growing back, settled placidly on Jude's forearm. Then they set off, followed at a polite distance by Swithin, the groom, on his own mount; he would watch the horses while Jude and Christina enjoyed the market. Christina glanced over her shoulder, annoyed at Swithin's presence. She was certain Lionel had insisted the groom accompany them to act as chaperone. For that very reason, Jude was delighted with the company. She figured that even the Lady Christina couldn't expect a declaration of love, or a marriage proposal, with a servant listening in on their conversation. And anyway, Jude was happy to know that if they were set upon by bandits, she and Percival would have some aid in fending them off and protecting the lady.

Jude rode slowly. Christina was not a natural horse-woman, and her lack of ease on horseback was magnified by her need to ride sidesaddle. She perched uncomfortably, most of her attention absorbed by the difficulty of staying mounted and keeping her skirts from flying around and exposing her legs. Thus, their conversation was minimal, covering only the beautiful summer weather and Christina's expectations for the kind of cloth she might find at the merchants' stalls. She did not say that she was hoping to find velvet and lace with which to make her wedding dress. Despite the way her horse jostled her and bumped along, Christina smiled at the thought of her imminent en-gagement. *Maybe today,* she thought, *if we can elude that stupid groom.* She knew that it was not up to her to accept a proposal—the proper thing would be for Lord Stephen to ask Lionel, who had been her guardian since their parents died. But she could tell Stephen that her brother would definitely accept the proposal, even if Stephen came from some insignificant manor east of nowhere. *Lionel wants his favorite sister to be happy,* she thought. She smiled again, though the horse jerked her head and almost pulled the reins from Christina's hands. It was a great relief when she finally heard the music and noise of the market and saw the crowd of people in the center square. Swithin carefully helped her down from the white mare and Christina dusted off her cloak, a demure smile on her face. She was ready.

Jude, however, hung back, leaning against the gray horse as if for safety. Such a crowd of people! And the noise—it was almost unbearable. She wanted to mount her horse again and ride back to the safety and comfort of Gwynna's castle, or even to the woods, where she had lived for so many days. Percival, his eyes covered by a leather hood, gave a discontented *"kek"* and flapped his wings. He didn't like the noise either, it seemed.

"Come, Lord Stephen. We have much to do." Lady Christina stood quietly, not showing her eagerness, while Stephen took his time handing the reins to the groom and coming to take her arm. He then reluctantly led her into the commotion.

They came first to the animal pens, which lay a bit on the outskirts of the square to keep as much of the dirt and smell as possible away from the center of the market. Jude admired the lovely specimens of long-horned goats and cattle, hares, pheasants, chickens, and long-haired sheep, but Christina just wrinkled her nose and stepped carefully until they were past. Next they arrived at the metalworker's stall, where the smiths, who stood making horseshoes, stirrups, tools, and armor, added their loud clanks to the din. Christina paused briefly to admire some pretty copper thimbles, but then passed them by when the worker gave her a price. Her brother had his own smiths and armorers; she didn't need to buy metalwork at the market. She did not even stop to look at the woodworker's stall, where fine doors, shutters, and furniture were displayed: she could see the silk merchants' tents up ahead. She tightened her grip on Jude's arm and hastened her step.

"Sweetmeats! Candied fruits, cakes, jellies!" a merchant called from behind his stall. Jude halted, entranced by the rich smells. She dug out a coin from her belt pouch and purchased two small spicy cakes, the tops decorated with melting sugar. Jude held one out to Lady Christina, but she declined. "How kind, Lord Stephen, but I am too excited to eat." That, and she did not want to dirty her hands before handling fine fabrics. Jude shrugged, and happily ate both cakes herself.

Entering the silk merchant's tent was like traveling to another land, Jude thought. The array of colors astounded her, as did the number and variety of people. The few market days in Nesscliff that Jude had been allowed to attend had been small, haphazard affairs, with a few skinny animals for sale, and perhaps one metalworker and one cloth merchant. The cloth for sale, though, had been coarse woolens for dresses and tunics, and linens to wear next to the skin. This being London on a major market day, however, the scene inside the tent was one of lavish display, with nobles dressed in multicolored finery bargaining with the merchants over bolts of fine material, their pages or servants waiting in the background to carry purchases away.

Christina paused at the entrance with a broad smile on her face. She took a deep breath—there it was, the smell of luxury! The spicy, nutty fragrance of the incense and candles burned by the traders from the East and other, European countries, ones much more exotic than her native England. She glanced at the merchants until she spotted a familiar face—Benedetto, from Venice. Pushing her way through the crowd, Jude following closely behind, Christina made her way over to Benedetto's table. She stepped around a tall, gaunt man with a white beard who was idly fingering the fabrics.

"Good day." She smiled at the merchant, lowering her eyelashes shyly. She knew that the Italian did not like forward ladies who discussed prices themselves. Lord Stephen would have to do the actual bargaining for her, when she decided on her selections.

"Good day, my lady," Benedetto replied in his heavily accented speech. "How may I please you today?"

Christina gave him her special shy smile. Foreigners were always so gallant. "I'm not looking for anything special," she lied. "We were just riding by and thought we would stop and see your wares." With raised eyebrows she glanced up at the tall man, who took her hint and ambled away in the direction of another merchant. She hated spectators when she was looking at cloth.

From underneath the table Benedetto pulled out a tightly wrapped parcel. "This is the very best," he whispered confidentially to Christina, who could hardly contain herself while he slowly unwrapped the package with loving hands. Finally he folded back the last sheets of linen and displayed the fabric: a velvet the color of cream, embroidered with gold thread and pearls. Christina gasped, and reached out to touch the material, thankful that her hands were clean. It was softer than anything she had felt before, with the pearls' delicate nubs, and the gold embroidery thick and cool. She had to have this fabric. Worn with a plain velvet kirtle on top, this fabric would make the most stunning surcoat and skirt. Christina could already picture the pearl-and-gold headdress to go with her veil. Unfortunately her hair would have to be covered—that was a necessity for a woman about to be married—but she knew that she'd still be the most favored bride London had ever seen.

" 'Tis pretty," Christina said in a slightly bored voice, once she had collected herself. Never, ever show a merchant that you're interested in his wares; that was one of the few helpful things her mother had ever taught her.

"Pretty!" Benedetto was aghast. "I sell three sheep to buy this fabric from the East, and you say it is just pretty?"

She shrugged, turning to Lord Stephen, who was standing behind her, craning his neck at the different stalls as if he had never been at a market before. Once they were married, she'd teach him not to gawk so. "Lord Stephen, what do you think of this fabric?"

Jude tore her eye away from the foreigners milling around the tent and focused on Christina, Benedetto, and the cloth. " 'Tis very ornate. What occasion would warrant such a fabulous costume?"

A bright blush crept over Christina's cheeks. How could he be such a simpkin? Couldn't he see that this would be perfect for a wedding gown? But she shook off the feeling—what did she expect from a boy, anyway? That he know all about fine fabrics?—and answered, "My feelings exactly. Benedetto, what other cloth do you have? Something more simple."

Shaking his head, the merchant pulled out other

bolts of fabric. Christina touched the silky materials, but her eyes traveled back again and again to the embroidered velvet. After she had spent a good quarter of an hour looking at the other cloth, she decided it was time for bargaining. "Lord Stephen," she called, trying to bring the lad back from whatever reverie made him look so distant. "Lord Stephen!"

"Hmm?" Jude was staring off in the distance, her heart pounding. It was only a glimpse, but she thought she had seen a familiar large figure over in the far corner of the tent. The height, the bulk, the same dark hair and beard . . . it looked like Smithy, her attacker! He—if it was actually he—didn't seem to see her. He had been whispering with one of the merchants, and then slipped out through a side of the tent. Of course he might be in London; why hadn't Jude allowed for that? What would she do if they met again? She couldn't challenge him to a duel—they weren't knights. Her hand traveled to the knife hanging on her belt, and she felt better then, knowing that this time she and Percival would be more prepared.

"Lord Stephen!" Christina hissed, exasperated. Jude snapped to attention.

"Yes, my lady?"

Christina composed herself and continued in her accustomed gentle voice. "It is time to make my purchases. What is your opinion?" She held up a plain

138

velvet, for the top of her wedding outfit, a bolt of lace for the veil, so delicately spun the pattern was hardly visible from two paces, a slate-colored silk for an everyday dress, and a scarlet taffeta she had no intention of buying.

Jude scrutinized the fabrics. She'd never had a gown made from any of these expensive materials; how could Christina buy so many at one time? "If I may say so without offense, m'lady, the red may not be as becoming on you as the others."

He had noticed her coloring! There may be hope for him after all, Christina thought. "You're right, Lord Stephen." She replaced the taffeta. "What are you asking for these three?" she asked Benedetto, gesturing to the remaining velvet, lace, and silk.

The merchant appeared to think carefully before naming his price of fourteen shillings. Jude blinked, hard. She could not remember anyone in her mother's household spending more than a shilling or two on dress fabric, and even that was considered an extravagant sum. But Lady Christina did not seem much perturbed. " 'Tis high," she commented, her hand returning to the scarlet taffeta she had already rejected.

"Yes, but worth it. The finest materials from the East. I would not travel all the way to London with lesser fabrics," Benedetto told her in a confiding voice.

Christina then shrugged, and half-turned away.

"I'm afraid fourteen shillings is too much for just three fabrics. My brother would not be happy." She took a step toward the opening of the tent.

"Wait, m'lady! I give you a bargain. Fourteen shillings for these three wonderful fabrics *and* the red cloth." He held up the taffeta invitingly.

"Lord Stephen?" she asked in a questioning voice. When was he going to take over this bargaining for her? It was shameful for a lady of her rank to be discussing prices with a merchant.

But all Lord Stephen had to say was, "I thought you did not want the red fabric." Then he continued to stare at the corner of the tent in that maddening way.

With a small sigh, Christina figured she must finish up the bargaining on her own. "Aye, I do not. What do you say to fourteen shillings for these three"—she pointed to the decided-upon materials—"*and* this one, too," she said, touching the gorgeous embroidered velvet.

Benedetto took a step back, aghast. "That fabric alone is worth fourteen shillings. It is the very finest silk velvet, and two people worked over a month to embroider it. Twenty-four shillings for the four fabrics."

"Sixteen."

"Twenty-two."

"Eighteen, and that is all I can offer—I have no more in my purse." Christina even went so far as to open her hanging purse and show Benedetto the coins. He couldn't know, of course, about the other five she had tucked inside her cloak.

The merchant considered. Eighteen was low, but he still would be making a healthy profit. "Sold," he announced, and bowed to the lady.

Smiling in relief, Christina emptied her purse onto the table. Benedetto scooped up the coins and poured them into his own pouch, which he tucked carefully inside his tunic. He then wrapped the four bolts of cloth in a linen wrapper and tied them up with a thick cord. Lady Christina gestured for Stephen to carry the parcel—the least he could do, she thought, after he abandoned her to buy on her own—and wandered through the tent, humming happily. There was nothing better than purchasing new fabric, especially ones so special as these.

Now that the important purchases were made, Christina decided to relax and enjoy some of the other stalls at the market. It always pleased her to pretend interest in an object and get the merchant's hopes up, only to walk away abruptly and onto the next stall. She waited impatiently while Lord Stephen delivered the parcel into the waiting hands of Swithin, the groom. Why had Stephen insisted that she wait in the silk merchants' tent? She'd already finished her business here. But he had been determined—nay, almost stern—in the urgent way he said she must wait for his return. As if something untoward would happen at a market in the middle of daylight. For the reverence of God!

Though annoyed, Christina waited. When they were married, she thought, he wouldn't order her about so. But for now, while they were still courting, it seemed proper for her to act the meek and yielding lady. She sighed with the weight of that role on her shoulders and tried without success to amuse herself, examining tapestries that were not so fine as the ones her brother's dyers and weavers could produce.

When Jude returned, she did not even notice that Christina was acting cool and distant—not that Jude would have cared particularly, even if she had noticed. While they wandered the rest of the market, Christina glancing at the abundance of furs and wines and spices, Jude was keeping a sharp eye out for Smithy. She was sure it had been he in the tent. But the large man did not appear again, and by noontime Jude had relaxed her vigilant watch.

The two dined at a long wooden table outside a cookshop, surrounded by other nobles. Another table held a pair of lawyers arguing in French, some wealthy merchants whispering about business, and three students conducting a lofty discussion in Latin about a particular passage of Virgil. The lesser merchants pausing for dinner had to eat standing by their booths, the tenant farmers sat in their wagons, the workers and serfs stood clustered outside the cookhouse doors or sat on the ground.

Christina dug heartily into their chicken-and-almond pudding, and drank deeply of her tankard of ale. Bargaining always made her hungry, and here she did not need to worry about her brother chastising her for poor table manners. Lord Stephen seemed more interested in staring at the ragged serfs than in conversing with her, so after she'd finished the main course, she helped assuage her hurt feelings with a plum tart.

Christina was right: Jude was paying little attention to her. Instead, she was thinking of the few markets she had attended in Nesscliff. They had been tiny compared to this one, but all the merchants, farmers, and serfs had eaten at table with the nobles. In Nesscliff, all knew that a market day was a time for celebration, and the nobles treated their serfs and vassals to a good meal, for that one day, at least. Even her stepfather had provided dinner for the peasants who worked his land. Jude shook her head at how unfeeling Londoners were. She hoped Kent would be different.

Christina was watching Maria unpack the parcel of fabrics when Lionel strolled into her chamber. She looked up, startled. Not only was it highly unusual for her brother to come visit her, but she really did not want him asking any questions about the price she'd paid for the fabrics. "To what do I owe this honor, m'lord?" she asked, rising from her little stool.

Lionel shrugged. "Can I not visit my sister without questioning?" he replied pleasantly, then turned to Maria. "Madam, will you leave us for a moment?"

With a curtsy, the gentlewoman left silently, shutting the door behind her. Lionel sat on the tiny bench that stood at the foot of Christina's bed. He looked uncomfortable, and Christina did not know whether this was because of the silly, low lady's bench he perched on, or because he had found out that she had spent eighteen shillings on cloth, or some other reason. She waited expectantly, but did not ask again his reason for coming.

Lionel stared out the window of his sister's luxurious tower room, his eye falling on the impressive courtyard below. Praised be God, fortune had smiled thus far on all other parts of his household; why did she withhold her gifts when it came to Christina? Finally he spoke. "Upon returning from the market, Lord Stephen told Lady Gwynna that he finds London an unsympathetic place. He was unhappy with the way the serfs were eating on the ground in the market square."

Genuinely puzzled, Christina asked, "Serfs? Why should he care about the conditions of serfs? They're property of the nobles whose land they work. What do the peasants matter to him?" She was relieved that the conversation had not turned to the price she'd paid for her fabrics.

Looking even more uncomfortable, Lionel continued, "It seems as though his father and stepfather had taken a personal interest in the well-being of the serfs, and fed them on market day. He said that his sisters even went to visit the cottages when workers were ailing or in childbed."

Christina shuddered at the thought. She often passed the cottages when she was out riding, but she made a point never to stop, nay, never even to look into the dirty yards and broken-down doorways, into the squalor that lay within. It was enough that the almoner collected the leavings from the castle meals and distributed them to the poor. "Why are you telling me this, brother? Are you telling me I would be more . . . attractive to Lord Stephen if I put an apron over my dress and went to minister to the serfs?" she asked with heavy sarcasm.

"What I'm telling you, sister, is that Lord Stephen was reminded by what he called the sinful spectacle of the marketplace that his true calling is music, and that within the fortnight, he must be on his way to serve his God, and the King, in Kent."

Within the fortnight! Christina sat bolt upright on her fussy little stool. Less than two weeks to get him to propose! She had been certain that first night when

145

they sang together that their betrothal would be announced on Lammas Day; but now Lammas was only three days away, and he was still planning on leaving London!

"Lady Gwynna told Lord Stephen how well we have always treated our serfs, giving them the uneaten dishes and bread from our dinners, and how they're allowed most of Sunday as a rest day each week, and holidays from Christmas Eve to Twelfth Night," Lionel explained. "But he said that was not his only concern; he felt that if he stayed much longer he would lose his inclination to become one of the King's Minstrels, and instead fall prey to the easy life a noble lives. He said that he did not belong here, living the life of aristocracy. A musician's life is his lot, and so it must be." The earl paused and looked at his sister. "Unless you can make him change his mind."

Christina rose and paced back and forth in the chamber. "What shall I do?" she mused aloud. "I have tried all of the usual methods that make a man fall in love—singing, smiling shyly at him, asking his advice. What more shall I do?"

Lionel stood up quickly and strode toward the door. "I don't care to hear more of your woman's tricks. I simply thought it right to inform you, as Lady Gwynna informed me, that Lord Stephen will be leaving within the fortnight. After that, he's lost—you cannot follow him to Kent. It would be forward, and

146

unseemly." He opened the door and called for Maria. "I now must return to the abbot. I trust you'll be at supper tonight, to help entertain him." It was a statement, not a question, and with that Lionel left the room.

Christina was not as disheartened as her brother would have expected. She still had a few of those "woman's tricks" to try, and unless those failed, she would not despair.

XI

THE POTION

*A*bbot Simeon gestured for the cupbearer to come and refill his goblet with the fruity red wine. They certainly didn't get wine like this at the monastery. He drank deeply, then set down his cup and again dug into the supper in front of him, eating heartily of the fat roast and the venison pie. Simeon had been unsure as to whether he wanted to take over the position of running the monastery when the old abbot died; he was but thirty, quite young for the job, and had been an Augustinian only for the past six years. There were older and more experienced monks to fill the abbot's shoes, but they had wanted Simeon. He was better at dealing with nobles, they said. They wanted to stay behind the monastery walls and pray, learn, and be self-sufficient, and were happy to leave any business with the outside to the more worldly Simeon, who came from a prosperous spice merchant's family. He had stood to inherit sizable properties from his father, but instead he renounced trade for a higher calling.

Maybe Simeon wasn't as pious as some of his brethren. At least he knew how to get the monastery's books in order (what a muddle they had been from the inaccurate calculations of the old abbot—may the Holy Trinity have his soul in Their keeping!), and how to enjoy himself while at table with an aristocrat like the earl. Not for Simeon the self-righteous attitude some clerics took while out in the world, eating only bread and water, wearing their hoods over their faces in mixed company, excusing themselves from dancing or music. He thought that behavior only distanced the clergy from others. He was an ambassador, and as such, he would do his best to represent the order without refusing any of his host's gifts. He gladly took another helping of lamb from the carver, and continued telling the story of his religious calling.

Jude ate heartily, too, while being thoroughly entertained by the abbot's story. Even with the top of his head shaved into the typical monk's tonsure, this cheerful man with his red, elfin face seemed less like a cleric than a merchant after a successful trade. Jude remembered her stepfather's ravings against the clergy, how he hated having to entertain the local bishop and

suffer a whole month's worth of sermons in one afternoon. In fact, Lionel's chaplain, one of the gloomier
specimens of his profession, was staring with a scandal-
ized expression at the way the abbot guzzled his wine.
He raised his eyebrows so high they looked as if they'd
soon disappear into his cap, but the abbot either didn't
notice, or didn't care.

". . . I'd already become a warden of the company,
so when I told the alderman I was leaving to become
an Augustinian, he said to me, 'George'—for that was
my name then, before I was called and renamed after
St. Simeon the Stylite—'George, a monk's life isn't for
you. You'll be there one week and miss your food and
drink, then don't come begging after me for your position back . . .'" Simeon paused to take another bite
of pheasant.

Christina looked helplessly at the round monk. How
soon would it be proper to leave the table? She knew
that her brother, as much as he might dislike a particular priest, always obeyed the strictures of tithing and
hospitality to the clergy. Picking delicately at the meats
on her plate—for not only was her critical brother
present, but she had so stuffed herself at dinner in the
marketplace that she had little room for supper—she
waited impatiently for a break in the abbot's story. She
had other business to attend to that evening.

As soon as she could leave discreetly, Christina bade

good night to her family, to Lord Stephen, and to the abbot, who was still licking bits of dandelion pudding off his spoon and regaling the table with stories. "You're leaving so soon?" Lady Gwynna asked, holding on to Christina's arm. Christina looked longingly at the door, her means of escape blocked.

"Aye, I'm so, so weary after today's excursion." She yawned delicately and covered her mouth with her one free hand.

"But you haven't yet told me about the market, and all your purchases! And how can you leave when the abbot is telling such fine stories?" She had noticed Christina's bored expression and the way she kept glancing at the doors of the great hall, as if she had someplace else to go. Gwynna might be acting the doting sister-in-law, but in truth she was still angry and wanted to repay Christina for the misdeed that had kept her from the market that day. Gwynna gestured for a page to bring another chair. "Sit next to me now, and tell me all about the fabrics you bought. How much did you spend? Come, you can tell me! I won't tell Lionel."

And that swilling monk won't have more wine, Christina thought. Not very gently, she pried her sister-in-law's hand off her arm and backed away, out of reach. "Nay, I'm afraid I'm too fatigued for a chat, though it does sound delightful. Good night, all." She turned and fled past the tables of guests and estate officials, past the marshall of the hall and the ushers, and out through the doors before anyone could stop her. She walked quickly to the great chamber, where she found Maria dining with the other gentlewomen. Catching her breath, she interrupted their chatter and told Maria it was time to retire. Together they ascended the main staircase and entered Christina's chamber, where the gentlewoman pulled off Christina's low leather boots and helped her off with the voluminous surcoat and tight kirtle. She drew the linen nightdress over her lady's head, and stood behind her, brushing out from its coils the long, golden hair, as Christina sat on her low stool, impatient but trying not to show it. Finally the nighttime rituals were done, and Christina sent the woman away. Leaving only one candle burning, Maria curtsied and left.

Christina sat down on her bed with a deep sigh. Finally, alone. Then, moving quickly, she stood and drew her boots back on, threw her cape over the nightdress, and took the candle to light her way. Drawing the door of the chamber closed behind her, she looked both ways down the long hall. In the distance, she could hear sounds of feasting from below, and Stephen's voice singing a merry tune. She felt a pang of regret that she wasn't with him but knew that her plan for tonight would make him love her even more than her singing had. Stealthily she crept down the main passageway, which was lighted at intervals by torches; then, as slowly and quietly as she could, she opened a heavy wooden door and slipped into the dark inner passageway that was used only by soldiers during a siege.

Feeling her way down the tunnel, she was glad of the high slits of windows that were spaced along the wall. The slender openings let in enough moonlight to aid Christina in making her way across the length of the manor in secrecy. She paused once, briefly, at a scuffling sound nearby. *What was that? Who was that?* She twisted around, being careful not to move so quickly that she'd extinguish her candle. The scuffling sound came closer. Holding her breath, Christina pressed herself against the cold wall, knowing that even if she put out the light, a person traveling the length of the passageway would find her. The tunnel was just too narrow, and the windows were too high to allow escape.

When two large rats scurried past, Christina gave both a shudder of disgust and a sigh of relief. She didn't like to share the tunnel with vermin, but it was better than being discovered by her brother. Picking up the hem of her nightdress, she hurried down the passageway, hoping she was in time.

Finally she came to another wooden door, identical

153

to the first. She pushed it open carefully, then gave a small jump as it creaked softly at her. She waited, but nothing else stirred. Slipping out of the passageway, she crept to a narrow stone staircase and made her way down slowly and with care, for there was no banister to hold. The staircase circled around twice before she reached the bottom. She peered cautiously into the dark, silent room, holding her breath. But she was alone. This entire tower of the manor was used only to shelter high-ranking guests and their households, and she had known tonight it ought to be empty. Christina held her candle out to the gloom and waited.

Moments passed, and she started to fear that she had come too late. But then she saw another light approaching, and let out the breath she'd been holding. "Agnes?" she whispered into the darkness.

"Aye, m'lady," replied a girl's voice. The candle came closer, and Christina now could make out the form of the young laundress. The girl pushed back her brown hood and stepped closer to Christina. "I was sure you wouldn't ha' come," she whispered with a smile, then turned and walked away. Christina hurried to follow. The girl led her through the series of dark kitchen rooms, then stopped when they reached the pantry and lit a torch with her own candle. The room seemed less gloomy when well lighted; Christina relaxed a little, and placed her candlestick down on the wooden slab that served as a workspace.

"So, m'lady, you wanted a love potion." Christina jumped at the girl's voice, and shushed her. "No one can hear, as far away as we are from the rest. And even if they was in the next room, they'd be too drunk to notice!" Agnes then leaned in close to Christina. "Do you want the potion or not?"

"I do," Christina breathed, still not wishing to raise her voice to full volume. "He must love me, or else he'll be gone within the fortnight. Do you have it?"

The girl nodded and pulled a small parcel out from the pocket of her apron. She untied a knot and laid flat the folds of cloth, exposing a fine ground powder the color of fresh mint leaves.

Agnes's mother, well known to be a witch, lived in a tiny, broken-down cottage on the road to the center of town. It would have been impossible to get to the witch's cottage, Christina had decided, but thought that maybe her daughter would do as well. And it seemed that the girl had succeeded. "What's in it, that makes it so green?" Christina asked, reaching out to touch the powder.

Agnes smacked her hand away. "Don't touch! 'Tis too precious to waste. And never you mind what's in it—that's my mum's business, not for you to know." Agnes regretted slapping the lady as soon as she had done so, but she was desperate to avoid unnecessary questions. Her mother had refused to make a love potion for the young lady of the castle, but Agnes

155

needed the money. So she'd decided to concoct a counterfeit potion and put the fee Christina paid toward a small dowry. Soon she could wed Ambrose the carter and be free of her mum's grasp, and their dreary old cottage.

Christina had never been hit before in her entire life, let alone struck by an inferior. For a moment she thought of calling her brother and ordering him to have this surly wench thrown into stocks, or even tortured, for her offensive behavior. But Lionel would ask too many questions, and furthermore, she needed that potion, so Christina quenched her anger and nodded obediently. "How do I get him to eat it? It doesn't look very appetizing."

Agnes sighed with relief and shook her head at the lady's ignorance. "You mix it with something tasty, that's how." The girl moved around the pantry familiarly, assembling ingredients. "You make him a caudle, and bring it to him at midnight." She broke several eggs, which she had lifted from the main kitchen, and mixed their yolks with honey and wine. "Then you must stay with him while the potion takes effect." She stirred in some bread crumbs, and put the metal goblet near the torch to warm.

"And how do I explain my visit?"

Agnes shrugged. "That's up to you. You love him, eh? That should be enough of a reason. And even if the potion doesn't take hold right away, you've been in his chamber, eh? If he's really a gentleman, he oughtn't leave you after you were compromised in such a manner."

Christina blushed at the implication but put the thought in the back of her mind for future consideration. If all else failed . . . "Will the potion really work?"

The girl shrugged nervously, feeling a tinge of guilt. "Usually Mum gives her word it will cause love, but this time she said something I didn't understand. She asked if it was for the young lord you rode to the market with, and I told her aye, it was. She said you shouldn't count on his love, that his heart went another way. She said no more, but there was a funny look on her face." Agnes omitted the fact that her mum had outright refused to make the potion. So she had made her own concoction, even though her mum had always cursed her for having no talent for potions and spells. She had simply crushed together basil, mint, and sorrel from the garden, and decided to hope for the best.

But Christina wanted guarantees. "I need a potion that will work!" she whispered furiously.

Unperturbed, Agnes moved the caudle away from the torch and stirred in the packet of powder, adding a scraping of cinnamon on top. "This is the best we've got. If this won't make him love you, nothing can," she lied, the lady's anger and desperation making Agnes bold once again. "Do you want it?" She held the goblet out toward Christina.

Curtly Christina nodded, handing over the five coins that she'd placed in her cape and taking the goblet in exchange. With a wide grin, Agnes pocketed the money and blew out the torch. "Best of luck to you, m'lady," she said with a curtsy. Christina felt the girl was being impudent in her manner, but there was nothing she could do about it. She had other things on her mind. It was almost midnight.

On the stroke of midnight, Christina tapped lightly and then pushed open the door to Lord Stephen's chamber just enough so that she could slip inside. She had the goblet tucked under one arm to keep it warm, and the candle in her hand. *Don't let me drop anything,* she thought, sending a silent prayer. She stepped into the room, now illuminated gently by the candlelight, and approached a surprised Stephen in his bed.

What in Mary's name is she doing here? Jude thought, panicking and sitting bolt upright, pulling the covers up over her chest. Only for sleeping did she remove the tight wraps that concealed her small breasts.

"Kek!" Percival, startled by being wakened so suddenly, flapped his wings, launched himself off the bedpost, and flew at Christina. For the reverence of

God, she'd forgotten about the blasted bird! She ducked, dropping the candlestick, which rolled on the stone floor and then went out. The goblet, though, she held tight. She stood as still as a stone until the falcon calmed and resumed his perch on the bedpost. Making her way by the light of the moon and stars that shone through the open casement, she walked to Stephen's bed.

"I thought you might like a warm caudle to help you sleep," she said, trying to pretend she had made her entrance as planned—graceful and alluring.

"I was already asleep," Jude hissed. If Lionel found out that Christina was here in the middle of the night . . . she shuddered, thinking of the consequences. "Don't you think you should go back to your own chamber?"

"Drink it," Christina said in her most seductive voice, handing Stephen the goblet. "I made it especially for you."

Figuring she wouldn't leave until the caudle was drunk, Jude downed the warm mixture in a series of gulps. It had an unusual taste, but was still warm and filling. Jude wiped her mouth with the sleeve of her thin nightshirt, then whispered firmly, "Delicious. Thank you, Lady Christina. Now it's time for you to return to your own chamber."

For the reverence of God! How long would it take

for that witch's potion to work? Stalling for time, Christina perched on the bed. Jude slid over, as far away as she could get. "I can help you fall back asleep," Christina suggested. "I could rub your back."

Wordlessly Jude shook her head. Should she chance getting up and showing Christina to the door? Though she was very slender, when her chest wasn't bound it was obvious that she wasn't a young man. Before Jude could make up her mind, though, Christina made up her own. *I'm not waiting any longer for some foolish potion,* she decided. She slipped off her boots, unfastened her cloak, and slid under the covers with Lord Stephen.

Jude gasped, and scrambled to get out of the bed. But before Jude could escape, Christina grabbed her wrist, pulling her close. "I know you love me, Stephen," she whispered. "It's time to show that I love you, too." Taking a deep breath for courage, she kissed his cheek gently.

Jude eased her head away. "Lady Christina, I'm afraid you're mistaken. Even if I did love you, I could not stay to be your betrothed. I have other commitments I must honor."

We'll see about that, Christina thought, and reached under the covers to embrace Stephen. Hugging him tightly, she expected to feel a hard, manly chest. Or at least a flat, boyish one. Instead . . . she jerked away in horror. Jude, meanwhile, was grabbing for the covers, hoping desperately that Christina hadn't seen or felt enough to know her secret for certain.

"What? . . . what is the meaning of this?" Christina breathed when she had found her voice. Shaking her head, she jumped out of the bed and, grabbing the covers firmly, yanked them away. Even with only the moon lighting the chamber, it was painfully obvious that Lord Stephen was a girl.

With a strangled cry, Christina threw down the bedcovers and fled from the chamber.

Jude was shaking. *Oh, Lord help me,* she thought. *What do I do now? If Christina tells her brother, he surely will notify my stepfather and send me back.* She couldn't even imagine the kind of punishment Lord Walter would think of for her. *I must leave—right now.* She leaped from bed and hurriedly started dressing, remembering to wrap her chest even though it would not be necessary to keep up the disguise if Christina exposed her secret.

She need not have worried about that. Christina, back in her own chamber, was sobbing tears of rage and humiliation. *How dare she make such a fool of me, pretending to be a suitor?* Her first thought was to tell Lionel, but she quickly banished that from her mind. Her brother would never let her live down the disgrace. He would make a mockery of her and her "suitor." She paced back and forth, vowing instead to have that damned wench drawn and quartered, or boiled in oil.

Jude was ready to go within minutes. All she needed was in a new pack; she took one change of clothes, and left the rest that Gwynna had so thoughtfully provided. She hated to leave her friend like this, without even saying good-bye, but knew it was her only option. Unless . . . unless Gwynna and Lionel were in separate chambers that night. It was chancy, but Jude knew how she'd regret leaving without an explanation. "Now, you be very quiet," she whispered to Percival, making sure his hood was on tightly. Taking her traveling pack with her, in case she needed to make a quick exit, she edged down the passageway, keeping close to the wall.

At Gwynna's chamber, she listened to make sure all was silent and then slipped in the door, sending a prayer that if Lionel were there, he would be soundly asleep. Inside the darkened chamber Jude paused at the door, waiting for her eyes to adjust, laying her pack on the floor and settling Percival on top of it. She strained to see the bed. How many shapes were there, one or two? It appeared to be only one, so she crept up to the shape under the covers, holding her breath and pausing after each step.

It was Gwynna, and she was alone. Jude let out her breath in a deep sigh of relief. Now the chore of waking her friend without getting the entire manor up. She remembered from their convent days how difficult it had been to awaken Gwynna for Prime and the first Mass of the day. Jude crouched on the floor, directly in front of Gwynna's face, and whispered her name.

No response. "Gwynna!" she tried again. She still lay sleeping. Jude shook her shoulder, which produced a low moan from the sleeper, but no sign of wakefulness. Finally, in exasperation, Jude gave Gwynna's head a violent poke with her finger.

"Ow!" Gwynna sat up and glared at Jude.

"Shhh!"

"Why did you poke me?" Gwynna whispered, then shook her head to help clear her sleepiness. "What are you doing here? You shouldn't be here, Jude; what if Lionel finds out?"

"*Christina* found out," Jude whispered back. "She climbed into bed with me."

"That shameless slattern! I knew she was up to no good," fumed Gwynna.

"Well, she got what she deserved, Gwynna. I don't think I've ever seen someone so angry. I'm afraid she's going to tell Lionel, and he'll send me home."

Gwynna nodded. "He's a good man, Jude, and a fine husband, but he would not approve of a runaway lass." She then noticed Jude's traveling clothes, and her eyes softened. "Are you going away now?"

Jude nodded. "I must. Before morning, before

Christina has the chance to tell her brother. But I needed to say farewell, and to thank you for your hospitality. You're my dearest friend, Lady Gwynna."

"And you're mine, Lady Judith." The two young women embraced tightly; then Gwynna pulled back with a sly grin. "I should say Lord Stephen instead. Now, how are you planning on leaving? The drawbridge is up. It takes six soldiers every morning to lower it, and they won't do that until dawn."

"By my Lady!" Jude breathed. She'd forgotten that this wasn't a simple manor house like the one she'd grown up in.

Gwynna's thoughts raced. It was only a couple of hours until dawn. "Go hide in the pantry," she said. "Put on a smock and dirty your face, and disguise yourself somehow as one of the kitchen boys. They'll be loading the abbot's cart up with goods come first light. I'm sure you can slip out then. And here." Gwynna grabbed her purse from under the pillow, and pressed ten pennies into Jude's palm. " 'Tis all I have."

Jude rewarded her friend with a smile. " 'Tis all I need. You always had the craftiest mind, m'lady."

Gwynna waved her away. "Go. You don't want to be discovered." She leaned over and kissed Jude tenderly on the check. "Godspeed. And good luck on your journey. You'll make a fine member of the King's Minstrels."

"Thank you. And you're already a fine lady of the

manor. Farewell." She squeezed Gwynna's hands once more, took up Percival and her pack, then stealthily made her way out of the dark room, down passageways and staircases, and into the dark series of kitchen rooms. She squeezed herself into what appeared to be an obscure corner and waited for the cock to crow.

Jude must have dozed, for the next thing she knew there was a shaft of sunlight in the room and the bustling sound of people coming from nearby. She sprang up stiffly, then ducked into the pantry's cold room, where meats were salted and roots and vegetables stored. "Shhh," she breathed to Percival, and carefully tucked him into her pack. The bird flapped his wings in brief protest, but did not utter a sound. Jude then pulled a blood-spattered apron from a hook on the wall and, tying it around herself and her traveling pack, slumped out to the main area of the kitchen, trying to look like a scullion.

Even though it was just past dawn, the kitchen was overflowing with people hurrying to load the wagons. The cook and his clerk, however, need not have been so worried to make haste; unlike his predecessor at the abbey, Abbot Simeon was not much concerned about reaching the monastery before chapter Mass. He knew they could manage without him for the morning, so he strolled around the courtyard, tranquil among the bustling servants, drinking his morning ale and munching on a nice slab of bread and cheese.

As Simeon watched the workers load up his cart and curry his horses, one of the kitchen boys caught his attention. Tall, blond, bent over in a peculiar way, so his face wasn't visible . . . he seemed to have a hunchback, or else was carrying something on his back. Simeon smiled when he finally recognized the scullion—it was that handsome musical lad who had tuned so well the previous night! Now, why was he out here in a bloody apron, hauling barrels of cider and salted fish?

Jude managed to avoid the cook and clerk, but didn't worry about the other servants. She knew they wouldn't bother her and risk getting into trouble by asking questions. The other kitchen boys knew she was a fraud, but shrugged their shoulders. The nobles were always doing peculiar things; why should they concern themselves with one more, especially if he was helping them carry these heavy loads?

When, for a brief moment, Jude was outside and saw no one watching, she jumped into the cart and wriggled herself tightly in between two barrels. It was very uncomfortable, and Percival, knocked around inside the pack, gave an angry squawk. Hushing the falcon, Jude eased him out of the traveling sack and held him close as more parcels were piled on the cart. Jude couldn't see a thing, and when the cart started moving shortly afterward, she was knocked back and forth into the hard barrels and had to brace her arms and legs to avoid being crushed by the heavy containers. *This is going to be a long ride,* she thought.

But then the cart stopped abruptly. Parcels were shifted away from the pile, and sunlight shone into Jude's hiding place. She tried to make herself even smaller, but then the final barrel was shifted to the side, and she was face-to-face with Abbot Simeon.

"Lord Stephen," he rasped, breathless from having moved all the heavy foodstuff, "won't you come join me up front? It would be much more comfortable."

Jude blinked a few times in the light, then sheepishly crawled out from the cart. She removed the dirty apron with as much dignity as she could manage, shoved the barrels into their proper places, and settled Percival back on her shoulder. Then she clambered up into the front of the wagon with the monk. She stole a sideways glance at Abbot Simeon, but he remained silent as he gave the reins a shake, inscrutable in his coarse woolen habit. Finally, Jude could stand the silence no longer. "You're probably wondering why I was hiding in your cart," she blurted out.

Simeon shrugged. "Nay, 'tis your own business, and none of mine." In actuality, he was immensely curious, but had learned long ago that the easiest way to make someone tell you something was to feign indifference. "I am sure you had a perfectly good reason for doing so."

Jude felt she owed the good-natured monk an explanation. He was, after all, harboring a fugitive. "It was Lady Christina," she confided. "She wants to marry me."

The monk paused. "And you don't want to marry her?" he asked with surprise. "She's a mightily handsome girl. Even an old celibate like me can see that," he said with a wink.

Blushing, Jude stammered, "Aye, she—she is. But I can't marry her."

Simeon looked at Lord Stephen sharply. The young man said that with such conviction . . . the abbot broke down and asked, out of curiosity, "And why ever not?" He wondered if this lad simply wasn't of the marrying kind.

"I *must* go to Kent. If they'll have me, I'll become an apprentice with the King's Minstrels. It's all I want, to play for the King, and be his emissary, traveling to spread word of his deeds, and teaching new ballads and tunes." As she said this though, with great vehemence, an image appeared in her mind of Robin, the comely young minstrel. Perhaps he, too, would be at Eltham Palace . . . she shook the picture out of her head. She was making this difficult journey because she wanted to be a musician, not someone's wife.

The monk nodded with understanding. He too had been called to a profession many of his family and friends thought was inappropriate. He hadn't been a man of great learning or piety before, and yet now he was the abbot of St. Clement's. Recalling the music of the night before, Simeon answered, "Aye, now I see. You are a mightily talented player."

Jude smiled at the compliment, then took Percival off her shoulder, checking to see how the falcon had weathered their time in the cramped back of the wagon. In spite of the close quarters, the bird seemed perfectly healthy to Jude, so she removed his hood and let him stand on her forearm. *He hasn't been fed yet this morning*, she thought.

As the monk and the girl rode in companionable silence, Jude waited until she spotted a flock of noisy starlings in a nearby tree. With a flick of her wrist, she launched Percival into the air. Amazed, Simeon caught his breath as the falcon shot off Jude's arm with incredible speed. Though the starlings hurled from their tree in a great chirping cloud, Percival was too fast. He circled once, then fell into a steep dive and snatched one of the birds right out of the air. Settling behind Jude, Percival devoured the starling with what Simeon thought was an admirable appetite. Intrigued, he asked, "How do you come to have such a fine bird? Usually peregrines are reserved for earls, not for young musicians."

Without thinking, Jude answered, "My stepfather is a baron. Percival was his."

"And he gave you the falcon?" Simeon asked, incredulously. A bird like that was not only an expensive treasure, he knew; it also conveyed the message that its owner was an aristocrat.

"Not quite," Jude admitted. She decided that she could tell this unusual monk at least part of her story. "My stepfather most decidedly did not approve of my dream of becoming a musician," she told him, knowing that was very close to the truth. "So when I ran away, he and his men gave chase, sending Percival to hunt me out of the woods." As she continued with the tale of how she had caught and won over the falcon, Simeon noticed what a fine knack the lad had for a story. *He'll make a fine musician and an entertaining minstrel,* Simeon thought. They could take him in for a week or two, although having secular guests who were not there on Church or monastery business was frowned upon. Even the pilgrims, who stopped at the monastery for a day or two on their way to Canterbury, paid well for the privilege. *But I am the abbot,* Simeon told himself with a wry grin. *This child needs a roof over his head until we can find him transport to Kent.* Without even realizing it, the big-hearted monk had taken on Jude as his responsibility.

Meanwhile, Jude was starting to regret her impulsive flight from Lionel's castle. How would Gwynna explain Stephen's absence? Jude fretted, feeling again the discomfort of keeping up the falsehood of being a boy. She smoothed down Percival's rumpled feathers and wished she could tell the abbot the truth.

She needn't have worried about Gwynna. Her old friend, though now a lady of great rank, was still the same mischievous girl from their convent-school days. Relishing the deed, she announced that morning, as they broke fast after first Mass, that Lord Stephen had been called away suddenly on urgent business, but she knew not where. A messenger had come before daylight, and the message carried up by one of the kitchen staff. Stephen had sent his hasty regrets, she told them, and then taken to the road at dawn. Gwynna looked at her brother and sister-in-law as she explained how sorry Lord Stephen had been to leave them this way, and how thankful he had been for their hospitality, and that he knew not when he would be in London again.

Lionel could tell there was something amiss with his wife's story. He scrutinized her carefully as she told of Lord Stephen's sudden departure, but did not question her. What did it matter, now that the lad was gone? With a sigh, he realized he must start again from the beginning with his search for a suitable husband for his difficult sister.

The difficult sister grew red in the face and could barely choke down her breakfast ale. Urgent business, indeed! She knew Gwynna was lying, but could do nothing about it. What would happen if she said she knew that "Lord Stephen" was really a girl? Her brother would demand to know how she had discovered that particular information, and he would shame her mightily, she was certain. Christina drew herself up and promised herself two things: that she would marry the next handsome man who paid her court, regardless of his age or station—as long as he was a man, and she would make sure he was; and that she would revenge herself on that fake Lord Stephen. Woe betide the accursed wench who had dared to make a fool of Lady Christina!

XII

ST. CLEMENT'S

Simeon and Jude reached St. Clement's Abbey in time to hear the bells ringing for high Mass. Bringing the wagon to a halt within the outer court of the monastery, Simeon called into the stables for aid with the horses and sent word to the kitchen that their tithe had arrived. He handed over the job of unloading the barrels to several servants and the recording of their contents to a novice. When he had finished delegating those tasks, he turned to Jude. "Lord Stephen, I must hurry now to the chapel. You may join us for dinner, which will follow the service, but our high Mass is for the brothers only. Would you like to wash before dinner?" Jude nodded, so Simeon called for another novice. "Crispin, please show Lord Stephen to a visitor's cell and provide him with some water and clean linen."

The novice, a youth a few years older than Jude, wore a black robe, but still lacked the monks' shaved tonsure. He bowed silently, then motioned for Jude to follow. He led the visitor through the courtyard and up a flight of stone steps into the guest house, where he opened one of the doors for her to enter. Still silent, he fetched a basin of water and a linen towel, placing them on a stone ledge in the bare room. The only furniture was a simple cot, and a wooden cross the only decoration.

The novice turned to leave without saying a word, but Jude stopped him. "Thank you, Novice Crispin. Abbot Simeon told me I might join him for dinner. When will that be, and where?"

"After the next bells, and in the frater. Go out to the courtyard again, turn left and take the path through the kitchen garden, into the passageway, then turn right. We all wait without the frater doorway until everyone has assembled, and then enter at the fraterer's signal." With a curt nod, Crispin then turned and left the cell.

Jude collapsed on the cot, then regretted having sat down so hard—unlike the feather-stuffed beds of Lionel's castle, the cot here had only a thin mattress, stuffed with straw, covering a wooden frame. Rubbing her sore backside, she sat up and tried to take stock of her situation. She could be in worse places, she knew, but a monastery would not have been her first choice. If it was discovered that she were a girl . . . she couldn't even consider the consequences. She would simply have to stay out of everyone's way—to avoid seeing any holy rite that would be a sin for her to witness—and to arrange transport to Kent as soon as was humanly possible. But Abbot Simeon expected her to stay for a visit, that was clear. He had seemed genuinely pleased at finding her in his wagon, and, Jude was sure, would be insulted if she stayed less than a fortnight.

She opened the tiny wooden window that overlooked the outer courtyard, to allow Percival freedom to come and go as he needed. "I think I shouldn't take you to the frater, whatever that is," Jude told the falcon, stroking his silky feathers. "If I can even find it." She wondered that the novice hadn't stayed to show her where dinner would be, but shrugged off the rebuff as clerical strangeness. Who knew what monks and other religious men might do? With a sigh, Jude washed her hands and face in the cold water from the basin, and combed her hair, noting that she was starting to look a little girlish again. With her belt knife, she hacked off the longer locks around her neck. Concealing the coils in her pouch, she planned a trip later that night to bury the hair in one of the gardens outside, or maybe in the privy. Then she wondered what kind of privy they had at the monastery, and what she would do if it was communal.

Jude shook her head violently from side to side, trying to dispel the doubts that came creeping up on her. *I've gotten this far, haven't I?* she thought. *I'm more than halfway. I'm not going to let a few monks prevent me from realizing my dreams.* Giving a final pat to her face with the rough linen, she left the cell in search of the frater.

It turned out that the frater was simply a large dining chamber, and that it wasn't so difficult to find after all. Leaving the guest house Jude spotted two other young men dressed like Crispin walking toward the main building, so she simply followed them. As the novice had said, they passed through an ample, neatly arranged kitchen garden, into a passage behind the kitchen, and stopped in a doorway where a large number of monks were congregating silently. Jude paused, taken aback by the many eyes staring at her. She tried to stand up straighter, even though what she really wished was to be able to shrink back into the solid stone wall behind her. The thought crossed her mind that she ought to have brought Percival with her—he always made her feel stronger.

Abbot Simeon rescued her from the curious stares of the brothers. "There you are, Lord Stephen," he called, making his way through the sea of black created by the robed monks. "Come, join me." He took Jude by the arm and led her into the frater, and up to the main table on a dais. A figure of the naked, suffering Christ dominated the space above, on a massive painted screen. Jude sat, feeling awkward and conspicuous sitting at the superiors' table, looking out over all the other monks who, in turn, seemed to be looking at her. And why was everyone silent? It had been quiet at the convent, too, but at the monastery she hadn't yet heard a single person besides Simeon and the novice speak.

The abbot waited until everyone was seated; then he recited a short grace in Latin. All mumbled an "Amen," after which the servitors came out of the kitchen, passing behind the rows of brothers at table to serve the first course. The appointed monk took his position at the frater pulpit, cleared his throat several times, then began a methodical reading from *Lives of the Saints*. " 'Saints Abdon and Sennes, Persian martyrs who professed their faith in Christ, died on this day in three hundred and three, in the year of our Lord. They were brought as prisoners to Rome and exposed to beasts, for having spat upon the images of the pagan gods. When neither lions nor bears would maul them, the Persians were hewn in pieces by gladiators. But the more their bodies were bloodied and mangled and covered with wounds, the more their souls were filled with divine grace and rendered glorious to the sight of Christ. . . .' "

The monk droned on throughout the entire meal,

occasionally repeating passages in a particularly loud voice. "Brother Thomas likes to make sure we've heard the most important points," Simeon whispered to her, "for our edification." He smiled. *Poor lad,* he thought. *Looks bored to death.*

Jude wasn't bored, however. She picked at her fish dish, wondering how the supposedly gentle monks could eat so voraciously while being told about mangled bodies and other atrocities. Saints' lives had been a part of her study at the convent, of course, but she wondered at these religious men who seemed more hungry than pious. The second dish was vegetables in a pastry, and Jude watched, again amazed at the monks' appetites. She didn't realize that, even though it was nearing noon, dinner was their first meal of the day.

When the last scraps of pastry had been eaten and the ale cups drained, the servitors cleared the tables and Brother Thomas finally finished the reading and closed his martyrology. As one, the monks from the row of tables stood and left the frater, off to wash their hands before None, their next session of prayer. Jude stood by her chair, uncertain of where to go next. "Lord Stephen," Abbot Simeon addressed her again, "may I now present you to our prior, our subprior, our precentor, and our sacrist?" He motioned to the other men who had sat at the main table. "This is Lord

Stephen, a talented musician, on his way to Eltham Palace." Jude, unsure of the proper behavior when meeting monastery superiors, simply bowed. The brothers nodded back and silently left the frater.

"They certainly don't speak much," Jude said, her low voice echoing in the empty hall.

Simeon laughed. "Nay, they let me speak for them. 'Tis one of my most important jobs." As they walked to the chapel once more, he explained how St. Clement's was one of the stricter Augustinian orders, in that they did not speak unnecessarily and ate no meat, only fish. "But we're still more worldly than the Cistercians, who are true ascetics, and the Benedictines, who wear hair shirts." Shuddering at the thought, Simeon continued, "I was called to this order by a force beyond my control; I was elected by them to be abbot because I never truly fit in with the silence of their monastic life. Or the dietary restrictions," and he winked at Jude, who smiled, remembering the monk's excesses at Lionel's table. "If I may be immodest, I was the perfect choice for abbot, one of them, but not averse—nay, even happy—to go out in the world and talk to the lords who tithe to us, and to host our visitors, and to do any number of other worldly duties that would disturb the serenity of the others. I'm different. I find my serenity just from being here, and do not need silence and fasting to feel the presence of God." The bells started chiming again, so with a quick nod and smile, Simeon disappeared into the chapel, leaving Jude standing in the cloister, wondering where to go next.

By winding through gardens and alleys, she eventually made her way back to her little cell. Feeling content to have a peaceful afternoon, she brushed Percival, then lay down on her cot and slept.

Jude's days fell into a pattern that ran parallel to that of the monks, whom she rarely saw except at mealtimes. The brothers started their day at midnight, with the Matins service, returning to bed after an hour and a half of prayers to sleep again until daybreak. The first two nights the ringing of the midnight bells woke Jude, but after that she didn't even hear them in her sleep. She rose at dawn, and went to the special Mass held for servants and guests. For two days there was another guest, a mason who came to repair the stonework in the bake house, but otherwise Jude was the sole outsider. Eating only bread and ale for breakfast, she too was quite hungry by the time dinner came around. After dinner she slept, as did the monks. Supper would be after Vespers, the six o'clock Mass, and bedtime shortly thereafter. In between meals, the monks worked and taught and prayed. Jude walked the expansive gardens, invented many new tunes on her pipes, hunted with Percival, practiced her reading in the library, and thought. For the first time since she had left her stepfather's home two months before, she had the leisure to think about her actions. Living in comfort, her needs taken care of by others, she needed only to abide by the constantly ringing bells. And even then—if she had chosen to skip morning Mass, or one of the meals, she knew Simeon would not have been dismayed. He understood the need for solitude and meditation in others, even if he required little of it for himself.

As it was, however, Jude sought out his company during the few times of day when their paths crossed. Jude spoke with practically no one else. The servants held her in too much esteem, thinking she was a lord, of course. The monks had no time for visitors, and the novices, whom Jude would have liked to get to know, avoided her. She was a little hurt by their coldness, but understood deep down that she represented to them the secular route they had left behind. Their lives were with the monks, and with the monks they stayed, not with some carefree visiting noble.

So Jude had much time for introspection, and as she spent the late-summer days in the bountiful gardens or unobtrusively watching the monks working the land or tending the animals, she wondered how she, the daughter of a minor landholder and his beautiful, but weak, lady had come to be staying in an Augustinian monastery. How she had come to travel by herself for weeks, living in the forest, crossing a land that was considered dangerous for men, let alone for a thirteen-year-old girl. How she had managed to avoid being slain by a bandit, or—even worse!—by a lady scorned.

In those quiet, ponderous days, Jude was unaware of how much she absorbed of the brothers' contemplative ways. She thought about her life, and her music. While music had been the driving force of her life since running away, she now saw how it had led her throughout all her days before that, as well. Even back in the convent, she remembered how music—and Gwynna—had made her life seem more special, somehow, charmed and apart from others. She wondered if her talent were a gift from God. Smiling wryly, Jude recalled the scene with that nun—Sister Brigid, she would never forget her mean old face—telling her not to be making a minstrel of herself, or think that she was any closer to God because of her skill. Well, maybe that despicable old nun had been wrong, she thought. Music had always been the only thing that made her feel holy. Religion was as much a part of her life as breathing: Mass, grace, morning and evening prayers, fasts and feasts and saints' days—they were a constant, a part of daily living. She thought about how Abbot Simeon served his God and King by being different from the other monks, not better or worse, but simply different. Can I serve by being different, too? Jude asked herself, sitting alone in the nave of the church and looking at the elegant lines and colors of the circular stained-glass window. Can I serve by becoming a musician, rather than a wife and mother? It was an incredible question to ask. The only girls Jude knew of who had refused the usual roles were the female saints, and most of them had come to violent and early deaths. And she knew she didn't want to be a saint; she wanted to be one of the King's Minstrels.

So in those quiet days, which stretched placidly toward the end of August, Jude finally reached some peace about her decisions. She hadn't known what a weight the guilt and worry had been until it was gone. And then, even with the knowledge that she still had many days of travel ahead of her, and after that, no certainty that the King's Minstrels would take her in, she felt free. Deciding that she would try to get transport from the next merchant passing through, Jude found Abbot Simeon in the chamber he used for monastery business, explained her need to leave soon, and thanked him warmly for his hospitality.

The abbot nodded. "It has been a pleasure hosting you, Lord Stephen. I've noticed how well you fit into the religious life. You wouldn't consider staying, perhaps?" he asked with a twinkling eye. "You're a bit young to be a novice, but we could start your education early."

Jude flushed at the compliment and briefly fumbled

for words. "I'm greatly honored by your offer, Abbot, but you know what my calling is. I must go, and serve in other ways."

Nodding, Simeon replied, "A fine answer, lad. I understand." He had known the youth would refuse his offer, but it was one he felt bound to make. A superior couldn't pass up the opportunity of a bright young man's joining their ranks; these days, there were simply too few who had the calling.

The abbot continued. "A blacksmith is coming tomorrow to repair the horses' shoes. If he's heading south, I'm sure we can provide him with some food or ale to make transporting you worth his while." Simeon stood and opened the wooden cabinet behind him. "I have a gift for you. 'Twas mine before I joined the order." He handed Jude a rote—a small, five-stringed harp. "I can't play music now, of course, not that I ever played with the talent that you do."

Jude protested, even as she cradled the lovely instrument in her arms. "Nay, 'tis too much. First shelter and food, now passage to Kent . . . the instrument is too dear. I've already taken enough."

Simeon waved his hand, stilling her objections. "It would give me great pleasure to know it was being played by someone who so loves his music. As repayment, you must stop here again and entertain me with songs and stories, once you are a King's musician. Is that enough compensation, that you will not grudge me the privilege of sharing some of our gifts with you?"

Even as she nodded her head, assenting to the generous offer, Jude inwardly protested. She hoped to find a way to repay the monks for their hospitality. She wasn't a knight—or even a lord, for that matter—but it wasn't right to accept so much without returning the courtesy.

The next morning, Jude woke at dawn, as usual. Looking out the small, high window in her cell, she felt regret that she was leaving this safe haven, but she was also eager for the last leg of her journey. She spent the morning tending to Percival and packing her meager belongings, wanting to be ready to leave at a moment's notice.

Waiting in the doorway to the frater before dinner, Jude scanned the room of men in black robes, looking for the blacksmith of whom Abbot Simeon had spoken. She was unrewarded until Simeon appeared, walking toward her with his guest. Jude stopped, dead still. She blinked her eyes, not believing the vision before her. The tall, beefy man accompanying the abbot was Smithy.

Jude cursed herself for not being prepared. Of course the man was a blacksmith; that explained both his name and his huge muscles. And she knew she had seen him in London—she hadn't been mistaken, then. In the seconds it took Abbot Simeon and his guest to reach her side, Jude was already forming a plan. She just hoped the abbot hadn't told Smithy too much of her intended journey.

Smithy was basking in the attentions of the abbot, feeling that finally he was being treated with the respect he deserved. Before, he had worked for unimportant landholders. He'd eked out a meager living shoeing their horses, but had received no gratitude or praise, and certainly never the hospitality of a meal. But his days in Waltham were now over; he had needed to leave town on short notice, in the middle of the night. It had been bad luck, getting involved with the daughter of Waltham's chief tenant-farmer. How was he to have known the maid was only eleven? She'd looked a robust thirteen, at least. Thankfully he'd been able to slip away from Langley, her father, before he came seeking restitution—or worse.

But that was all over, and he'd had the good fortune to come to London. He'd done well at the marketplace, selling the bracelet. With that money, he'd been able to buy a new set of clothes, some decent boots, and fix up his wagon. Now he looked every bit the respectable blacksmith, who could travel to abbeys and manors and be treated with the esteem that was his due. And this abbot certainly was treating him well, inviting him to join the monks at dinner. Not that the quantity of food would be what he was used to, but the honor was there just the same.

All puffed up with his newfound respectability and the care of the abbot, Smithy made his way through the congregation of monks. When he noticed a slender, blond figure staring at him with a mixture of wrath and fear, his features clouded with confusion. Who was this lad looking at him so strangely? Then, with a shock of recognition, Smithy realized that this was the boy whose bracelet he'd taken. God's wounds! Why hadn't he killed the knave when he'd had the chance?

"Lord Stephen! There you are," the abbot called out jovially. "This is the man who can provide you with transport south. Smithy, this is the young lord who I know will entertain you in your travels. Lord Stephen, I'll leave it to you to tell Smithy where you're going, and why. 'Tis a marvelous story, one to be told by you and no other. The two of you will need to observe the silence at dinner, of course, but you'll have plenty of time to tell tales after." He steered them into the frater, sitting both of them at the honored table on the dais. Normally, a laborer would not have joined the monks at a meal—instead he would have been fed in the kitchen, with the servants—but in this case, the abbot was asking a favor and wanted to be as hospitable as possible.

Jude shook slightly as she was seated next to the man who had beaten her and left her for dead not so many weeks before, but she steeled herself with the knowledge that this time she was prepared. She was grateful for the pack she had carried with her, and the foresight that made her leave Percival waiting, hooded, in the window of the corridor outside the frater.

Smithy gulped his ale down, she noticed, and was sweating quite profusely, sneaking glances at her out of the corner of his eye. *I could give him up to the monks,* Jude thought, then dismissed that idea. She had a plan already formed. The only question was how to carry it out and not soil her name. Of course, it wasn't really her name, but she did not want to affront Abbot Simeon's generosity and leave without an explanation. Her thoughts churned, working out details, as she chewed and swallowed food that might as well have been hay, for all she tasted it.

The appointed monk was reading an account of the day's martyr, St. Hippolytus, who was torn apart by horses. " 'They took a pair of the most furious and wild horses that could be found, and tied a long rope between them to which they fastened the martyr's feet. As he was dragged violently over rocks and briars, his blood poured profusely over the land. The faithful followed, weeping, to gather his flesh and limbs. . . .' " When Smithy paused in his feeding to look up at the brother who was so forcefully reading about the saint's death, Jude took her chance. Quickly and furtively, she leaned over her plate and dumped a handful of herbs into the blacksmith's drink. By the time he looked back to his meal, Jude was eating placidly, as if she'd never moved. She thanked the Lord that through all her travels and mishaps, she hadn't lost the powders Goodwife Middy had given her. It was the mixture wrapped in black cloth that she poured into Smithy's drink, and she sent a silent prayer, hoping that the old woman had been right saying that the potion would disarm an enemy, but not kill him.

Smithy, disgusted at the reading, took another large gulp of ale. If it tasted different to him, he didn't seem to mind, because he drained the cup dry. Simeon, always a good host, filled the cup again, then watched with concern as the enormous blacksmith turned white. Smithy grabbed at the table and tried to stand, then collapsed onto his trencher, his head landing in the remnants of his cheese.

"Brother Francis! Where's Brother Francis?" Simeon called, standing and searching for the monk with the most knowledge of healing. Had the blacksmith drunk too much ale? He looked like he could put away barrels at a time, but appearances could be deceiving. Simeon wrung his hands as Brother Francis and several other monks hauled Smithy out of his food and carried him to the infirmary. Only then did the abbot notice that Lord Stephen was gone.

At the first sign of commotion, Jude was out the door of the frater, through the long hall—where she grabbed Percival and planted him solidly on her shoulder—and into the courtyard. By the time Smithy was in the infirmary, she had told the stable groom about the emergency that called her away, and that required the blacksmith's wagon and horses. As she flicked the reins, sending the horses into a fast canter, she thanked her quick tongue and quicker reason; she would be far away when the groom realized he had been tricked.

Frightened that Smithy would come after her, Jude rode all out for nearly an hour, then had to slow the horses for a rest. She couldn't have known that Smithy would be laid up for hours, vomiting mightily, numbed out of his mind. But Jude did know that she had one more item of business to take care of. Still looking nervously over her shoulder, she stopped on the outskirts of the first town she reached. Jude searched the wagon, finding—as she expected—no money, and no bracelet. Having little need for the blacksmithing tools, she left them, but gathered up two knives and a warm blanket of coarse wool. She deliberated, then decided to leave a sturdy ax behind: it might come in handy, but was too heavy to carry comfortably.

Jude unharnessed the pair of horses from the wagon and led them into town, looking for the telltale ivy branch that marked a tavern. When she found the first ale house, she tethered the horses outside, brushed off her dusty tunic, and stepped into the gloom. Its being the middle of a working day, the tavern was empty but for two bailiffs sitting in a corner, negotiating over a tankard of beer. Jude left and continued to the next ale house, where she spotted a young peasant boy sipping a tankard of cider, joking with the tavern maid.

Jude approached the lad and made a point of sitting beside him. "That cider looks good. I'll have some, too," she told the maid, placing a penny on the wooden counter. The cup presented was none too clean, but Jude gulped the strong drink gladly, knowing it would calm her nerves.

"You're not from town, are ye?" the boy asked curiously. He was younger than Jude, she guessed, but tall, and had intelligent dark eyes. His question was phrased in a friendly tone of voice, and Jude answered gladly.

"Nay, I'm on my way home, from a long journey. And I'm troubled," she told him, emptying her cider cup and pushing it to the maid for refilling.

"What troubles you . . . m'lord?" He guessed the lord part—the falcon tipped him off, as did Jude's clothes. They were travel-stained, but of good quality, and Jude's leather boots must easily have cost more gold than his own family would see in a year.

Jude smiled at the title. It was a relief that she still passed as a male, and she was thankful that she'd cut her hair again. Pausing a moment, she then turned back to the intelligent lad. "I left a friend without saying farewell. I needed to be on my way again, but now I regret my hasty departure."

"Who did you leave?"

"Piers, quit yer nosy questions," the tavern maid called to the boy in a thick country accent. "Yer harassing the customers."

"Nay, 'tis fine," Jude called back. "Perchance the lad can help me." She turned back to Piers. "I left a man named Brother Simeon. He's the abbot of St. Clement's Monastery, outside the walls of London. He was called away on religious duty, so I could not take my leave of him properly."

"And how might I help you?" the boy asked, wondering what kind of deal he could strike.

Sipping her second cup of cider, Jude told him. He could earn a handsome knife, Jude said, showing the nicer of the pair she had taken from Smithy's wagon, and two pennies. She placed the knife and coins on the counter, knowing the peasant lad would rarely have had any money of his own. Serfs dealt almost entirely by barter, trading services or goods. All he needed to do, she said, was take a letter to the abbot, and leave it with a stable groom.

"A groom? Why not the abbot himself?"

"He might still be away. And he's a very holy man, Piers, not to be bothered lightly. Besides, the groom would take your horse."

"My horse!" the lad scoffed. As if his father would let him take one of the horses. They had only two, and both were needed to pull the plow.

"Aye. To show my thanks to the abbot, I'm sending one of my horses. Riding, you can make it to the abbey by midafternoon, and then walk back before dark. If you leave right away."

"A deal!" Piers cried. "Let me just run and tell my father. I'll be back before your letter is written!" He jumped off the bench and ran out to the fields, eager to show that he hadn't just been flirting with Alice, the tavern maid, again—this time he'd been earning some coins.

Jude hated to use the parchment Goodwife Middy had given her, but it was the only writing surface available, and she no longer needed the map to London. Though she doubted the lad could read even English, she wrote in French. There was always a chance the letter could fall into the wrong hands, and as she had no wax to seal the note for privacy, she wrote very briefly:

To Abbot Simeon of St. Clement's Monastery. Right worthy and worshipful sir, accept my deepest apology for the manner in which I departed. The blacksmith is an old foe. I could not risk harm again. Thank you for all you have done. Almighty God bless you and keep you in his governance. Written in haste this XIIIth day of August, anno Domini 1331.

She squeezed the name Stephen at the very bottom, then folded the note in a scrap of cloth, to avoid smudging the charcoal letters. As he had promised, Piers was back by the time Jude had finished writing, and she handed over the note, knife, coins, and horse with no qualms. The boy seemed honest enough, and she'd detected no gleam in his eyes that said he even considered running off with the horse and selling it, rather than bringing it to the abbey. They parted company cordially, Jude setting off south on her horse, Piers going north on his.

XIII

ELTHAM PALACE

*J*ude should have arrived in Kent within a matter
of days, even though the scrawny workhorse she
rode walked hardly faster than she could have on her
own. But her kind nature got the better of her. She had
sheltered with a peasant family in Yalding. The father
had a broken arm, and the mother four children and a
new babe to care for.

Thus, Jude decided to stay and help the older boys
harvest and thresh the grain, and start sowing the field
with the help of her old horse. When she wasn't too
weary from her day's labor, Jude played and sang for
the family, perfecting the songs she hoped would gain
her entrance to Eltham Palace. The eldest girl, Maud,
had a lovely voice and an ear for tuning. Jude left her
the precious little harp that had been a gift from Abbot

Simeon, and gave the old horse to the family to keep. She had felt at home in their cramped and smelly hut, but after the Michaelmas festival, Jude knew it was time to leave. She had her own path to follow.

It was a tired, hungry, and bedraggled figure who reached Kent several days later, on the Feast of St. Francis. No bandit had beset her on the roads, but there were few taverns—and even fewer barns—in which to spend the night, and Jude had slept in the forest, getting soaked by the frequent rains. She had eaten fruit already fallen from trees, and nuts, which were plentiful, but not much else. Twice she cooked and ate birds Percival caught, but the other nights were too wet to light a fire. She huddled in the shelter of a large rock or tree and shivered even as she slept, waking to gnawing hunger. But even in her misery she felt a kind of elation. She was almost at the end of her journey.

And, when she reached the palace, she knew the months of travel and lies and uncertainty had been worth it. She stood outside the gatehouse and gaped, her heart swelling. Jude felt as if she had finally reached her home. With confidence, she strode up to one of the many soldiers guarding the bridge. "I'm here because I want to become one of the King's Minstrels. To whom shall I speak?"

The guard snorted, taking in the boy's mud-stained clothing and pinched face, even while being intrigued by the peregrine falcon on his thin shoulder. "Away, lad." He shooed Jude with an armored hand. "Sir William cannot be bothered with the likes of you."

Deflated, but still resolute, Jude pulled the pipes from her pack and began a merry, but difficult, tune. Jude didn't know where she got the strength to play with all her skill. After days of grueling travel, she knew she had not come these hundreds of miles to be turned away by a soldier.

The soldier thought better of his decision when he heard the lad play. He had to admit there was some talent there, which perhaps Sir William should hear. And so Jude finally gained entrance to Eltham Palace, and an audience before Sir William, the master himself.

Jude's audition seemed to pass by in seconds. *I prepared for this for months,* she thought, *and now it's suddenly over.* She played an intricate tune on a borrowed harp, then sang the King Arthur tune she had learned so long ago at her stepfather's manor. The joy and relief that swept over her when Sir William said she could stay was like nothing she had ever experienced before. It was like coming home, she thought, but a home where she was cared for and wanted, rather than the reality of her home in Nesscliff, where, at least since her father's death, she had felt unneeded and in the way.

Sir William led Jude from the small chamber where she had auditioned into a stone passageway, taking her through the kitchens in search of something more to eat than the bread and cheese he'd provided when she first appeared. "This is Jude of Winchcombe. He's going to be joining the apprentices," he said, introducing Jude to a tall, dark woman who was overseeing the work of at least twenty cooks and servants. "This is my wife, Lady Margaret." Jude was surprised to see a lady in the kitchen, but as she bowed to Lady Margaret, the woman's natural manner showed her as one who would be at ease anywhere.

"And he looks like he could use a good meal," Lady Margaret said with a laugh and a kind look. She watched indulgently as Jude devoured a juicy slice of meat and some dark bread, and drank a full goblet of warm caudle. Her stomach full for the first time since Michaelmas, Jude was overcome by fatigue. She tried to stifle a yawn as Sir William explained what her duties would be for the next few days, but the combination of her exhaustion from traveling, the relief at being able to stay, and the warm food and drink made her almost bleary with fatigue.

Lady Margaret cut Sir William off in his instructions. "The lad's already half asleep," she chided. "Why don't you show him the lodgings? He can get started on lessons tomorrow. And ask Lucas to take that handsome peregrine out to the mews. We can't have falcons in the apprentices' chambers, I'm afraid."

Smiling, Sir William agreed. "I'm just pleased to have such a talented addition to the company." He slapped Jude heartily on the back once more, waking her briefly from her stupor. She stumbled after Sir William, following him through more long corridors, stopping only long enough to hand Percival over to a servant lad who seemed thrilled to have the noble bird under his care. *I'll never remember how to get back,* Jude thought, but the idea stayed in her weary mind only for a moment.

William stopped in front of an imposing door. "These are the apprentices' lodgings," he told her, knocking and then entering. He addressed a person within. "Glad you're here. There's someone I'd like you to meet. This is Jude of Winchcombe. He's traveled all this way on his own to become one of our apprentices, and not in vain. Though young, he has more talent than I've seen in many years." Sir William gestured for Jude to join him in the chamber.

So tired she could barely move her feet, Jude followed Sir William inside. "Greetings, Jude," said a strangely familiar voice. Jerking her head up, Jude looked into the shining green eyes of Robin, the minstrel she had met so many months ago—the minstrel who had first given her the idea of running away.

Jude's mouth gaped open, and she was unable to

return the greeting. William, attributing the lad's silence to fatigue, continued. "Robin has just returned from a long journey himself and is now taking a turn at teaching the apprentices. He'll be your direct master here for the next several months, until another minstrel returns and it's Robin's time to travel once again."

Does he recognize me? Jude asked herself. Looking up at the young minstrel who smiled so warmly, she finally stammered, " 'T-Tis a pleasure to meet you."

"Nay, the pleasure is all mine," replied Robin. "Welcome to Eltham Palace, Jude of Winchcombe. Welcome to the King's Minstrels."

XIV

GILBERT

*L*istening to the rustle of bodies around her, Jude realized that keeping her female identity a secret would be no easy task. Gilbert, another apprentice, shifted noisily in his cot just inches away from hers, groaning as he turned. Even the peasant's hut in Yalding had been more private than the apprentices' lodgings at the palace. Maud's family had all slept in their clothing, and washing, when it happened at all, was usually restricted to hands and faces. But the apprentice boys and young men were less modest, and Jude had burned with shame as they stripped off tunics and breeches and climbed shivering under feather quilts. She felt like a bumbling country fool getting into bed with all her filthy clothing still on, but what choice did she have? Lady Margaret had said they'd find more decent attire in the morning.

In Yalding, there had been no real privy, just a trench on the far side of the field, and Jude had taken care to visit it only in darkness or when there was no other person around. But now, from her room deep within the palace, it was impossible to make her way outside to relieve herself. At night the boys used clay jugs, and emptied them into the privies in the morning. Jude squirmed uncomfortably under her quilt, crossing her legs and wishing the other apprentices would fall asleep so she could finally use the earthen jug. She felt crowded, hot, and worried; it was going to be a long night.

"Will we meet the King?" she whispered to her fellow apprentices the next morning in the great hall.

Gilbert snorted, and almost spat out a large mouthful of ale. "Meet the King! Listen to this, Harold!" he called across the trestle table. "The new apprentice wants to know if he'll be meeting the King!" Turning back to Jude, he spoke with heavy sarcasm. "Aye, King Edward will be joining us shortly for cold mutton and cider. He always breaks his fast with us lofty apprentices, right after morning Mass." Shaking his head, he turned back to his food.

Jude, face burning, focused on the bread and cheese in front of her. The hall itself was overwhelming in its size and noise level. It was a beautiful room, with rich tapestries on the walls and the most intricate design of beams for the ceiling. But Gilbert had chided her for "gawking like a serf at a trained bear," so she kept her head down and tried not to call any more attention to herself.

Another apprentice—she thought his name was Matthias—nudged her leg under the table. "The King's been traveling in France and Scotland for months; his brother John is regent in his absence," he whispered, keeping a close eye on Gilbert. "Duke John is often at Eltham, but is meeting with the councils in London right now. Even when he or the King are here, though, they eat up on the dais"—he gestured discreetly to the raised platform at the far end of the hall, near the roaring hearth—"and pay no attention to us. We bow if they walk by, of course, but no apprentice I've ever heard of has actually spoken to the King or his brother, and I've been here nigh onto two years."

Jude nodded, but didn't trust herself to speak. When Lady Margaret appeared at her side, she left the table with great relief and followed her into a small chamber next to the kitchens.

"You can wash here," Lady Margaret gestured to a basin and cloth set on a low table. "And I've lain out some clothing for you to try. It isn't new, I'm afraid, but it's a sight better than what you've got on. When

203

you've finished, report to Sir William for instruction." With a benevolent nod she shut the door behind her.

Shaking, Jude leaned her head against the cool wall and tried to collect her thoughts. It was the first time she'd been alone since she had arrived, and her head was spinning from all the new ways to learn and new people to meet. Gilbert looked so much like Gwynna! With his red hair and mischievous grin, she had thought he'd be an ally—no, a friend—because he reminded her so of her dear Gwynna. But instead he'd mocked her at every opportunity, drawing attention to "the new apprentice's" shabby clothes and country ways. *He, too, must have been new here once,* thought Jude fretfully, though she guessed he was several years her senior. He probably didn't remember what it was like.

With a sigh, Jude stripped off her clothes with great relief and scrubbed at her grimy hands and face with the cloth. Her body wasn't too dirty, protected as it had been these past months by her clothes, so she gave it only a cursory wiping before trying on the breeches and tunics lain out before her. The third set of breeches were finally long enough, and she settled on a dark tunic to help conceal her bosom. Her breasts seemed to be a mite bigger, but she ignored the thought and simply bound them tighter, convinced that no one would think of looking twice. Thus clean and dressed, she took a deep breath and went off in search of Sir William.

She found him in a lovely octagonal wooden room behind the apprentices' lodgings. "Come in, come in," he called impatiently as she dallied by the door, peering at the five youngest apprentices who sat in front of the music master. "This is Jude, from Winchcombe. He'll be joining you now for lessons. Jude, these lads are Richard, Matthias, Roger, Will, and John."

John, clearly the youngest of the group, spoke in a clear, melodious treble. "Call me Jankin. There's a Master John already, and another apprentice John, whom we call Jack."

Jude smiled at the friendly boy and took the seat Sir William offered. "Now, Jude, I know of your skill on the pipes and the harp. Can you also play the lute and the rebec?"

"The lute, M-M-Master," she stammered. "I've seen a rebec, but never played one."

Handing her a slightly battered pear-shaped instrument, like a lute but with strange ridges across the fingerboard, William instructed her, "So, now we'll proceed with our lesson on tuning string instruments. Roger, will you take the rote, and Jankin, pick up the mandolin—no, that's the mandola, take the smaller one instead—and Richard . . ."

———

It seemed like a week passed before Jude could take another breath. Each day was the same: morning Mass in the chapel; bread, cheese, and mutton in the great hall; then lessons on playing instruments and reading and inscribing music. Dinner in the great hall was followed by scholarly instruction with Master Hal in a freezing room that looked out onto the great court and the gatehouse. When the sun was high up in the sky, and all the apprentices shifting on their wooden benches and yearning for respite, it was time for singing lessons, with yet another group of apprentices. It was dark when they had their light supper and climbed exhausted into their cots in the crowded lodgings. After that first uncomfortable night, Jude was simply too tired not to sleep the moment she crawled under her quilt. The sabbath day came as a welcome relief, and Jude gladly spent the morning in chapel, resting as she prayed, and then the afternoon outside and in the mews with Percival, whom she had been sorely neglecting.

Jude was not ranked with the youngest apprentices for long, at least with her instrumental lessons. By her third day at Eltham she had been moved to the highest level to work with Robin and the older apprentices. She didn't understand why, but just being in the same room as Robin made her flush and stutter. It didn't help that Gilbert was in that group, too, and taunted Jude constantly about any mistake.

As for singing Jude knew she was ranked in the middle of the apprentices. Her alto was pleasing and clear, but the boy sopranos—like Jankin—were trained and praised the most, even though their talent lasted but a few years. The older lads and young men were trained, too, the basses, baritones, and tenors; but the altos whose voices hadn't changed yet were simply extra bodies for the chorus. Jude didn't especially mind, however, since she knew that playing was her gift, and singing a mere tool to accompany it.

"He keeps saying I'll have such a strong baritone when my voice changes," she muttered to herself one evening as she dragged herself to the great hall for her last meal of the day. "But Master John will have to wait a long time for that!"

To Jude's great shame, she was the worst in her scholarly class—poorer even than little Jankin at Latin, science, and arithmetic. Her convent training, though adequate for a girl, had provided only minimal experience with long translations or sums. While Jude conversed fluently in courtly French, and could even write a letter in almost-proper Latin, she was left humbled and frustrated the first time Master Hal handed her a parchment. "From the Roman philosopher Seneca," he boomed with his imposing voice, so startling in such a gray, little man. He watched as Jude picked out the familiar few words from the complex text, moving her lips and trying to make sense of the passage. "You can

207

do a word-for-word translation, can't you?" While apprentices much younger than she were already studying rhetoric, logic, and astronomy, Jude was still struggling with translations from her Latin primer. It was a humiliating experience for someone who had always been a satisfactory student, and she cursed the nuns from her old convent school, and her parents, and the whole system that did not give girls an equal education.

"My father did not believe in schooling," Jude lied to Master Hal. "I had occasional lessons from my father's clerk, when he took pity on my untutored state, but no formal education. Forgive me my ignorance, sir. I shall try harder."

"No formal education, indeed," Hal complained to Master William one evening while they enjoyed a fine French wine in one of the court rooms—privileges allowed when the King and his regent were away. "That new lad you took in is as stupid as a bag of stones."

William sipped his wine meditatively. "He speaks well enough."

"Aye, he speaks enough for two apprentices, at least when trying to justify why he can't tell euclidean geometry from Ptolemy's map of the universe. I can't teach him."

"He's quick enough with his music studies. Learning to write music and all that. He can even tune his instruments by ear."

With an impatient shrug, Hal asked, "And what of his scholarship? Can we really send out a minstrel who is so woefully ignorant? What message will that send to the lords, if an emissary of the King's is nearly as illiterate as a peasant or a girl?"

"He has many years before he'll be the King's agent. Just do the best you can with him, Hal, for I won't cast out a natural musician for the lack of a little Latin. Another drop of wine?"

Jude, of course, knew nothing of this conversation, or of the many other whispered discussions that took place about the newest apprentice and his strange ways. Instead she was focused on keeping her secret, not dishonoring herself constantly in her lessons, and finding a time to speak with Robin alone. All three tasks proved nigh impossible.

She met daily with Robin, and yet he was as unavailable to her as he had been back at her stepfather's manor. Since the first day, he had not acknowledged in word or deed that he saw her as anything but another apprentice. *He must recognize me,* she thought. *Why doesn't he say anything? What if he truly does not know who I am? Should I reveal myself? Will he keep my secret?* Jude's thoughts were in such turmoil that every lesson with Robin filled her with anxiety. And yet, despite the apprehension she felt in his presence, the hours when Jude did not see Robin were even worse. Although she told herself it was the music lessons she anticipated with such eagerness, in her deepest soul she knew it was Robin she could not wait to see every morning, Robin who haunted her thoughts during the day and dreams at night. *If only I could speak with him alone!*

It was almost three weeks before an opportunity finally arose. As Jude sweated over a translation of Virgil that she hadn't been able to finish during her lessons with Master Hal, a breathless Jankin burst into the apprentices' lodgings. "Master Robin wants to see you," he announced.

Gilbert, idly throwing dice with a few of his friends, looked up and grinned. "Didn't I foretell it?" he said to no one in particular. "The masters would never let such a poor specimen stay here. Why, even wee Jankin is better at his lessons, not to say being more of a man." He laughed and returned to his game, while Jankin blushed a deep crimson and returned to the younger boys' chamber.

Thrusting her wax tablet and stylus under the cot, Jude rose and sought out Robin, heart pounding and mouth dry. Masters and apprentices rarely saw one another after evening prayers, save for the occasional instrumental or choral performances Master William organized on a saint's day. Only once before during Jude's stay had an apprentice been called from lodgings to speak with a master—when Alfred, master of instrument making, discovered that Roger had crushed an almost completed double flute by sitting on it accidentally and then had tried to hide the evidence to escape punishment. Poor Roger—a pale, pasty lad with a great talent for losing and breaking things—had been sentenced to bread and water rations for two days, not for the breaking of the flute, but for the concealment of his crime.

I haven't broken anything, Jude thought as she hurried from one room to the next. *And my lessons haven't gotten any worse, though they haven't gotten much better, either.* That was as far as she got before reaching Robin's chamber. After futilely trying to slow her breathing, she knocked and was told to enter.

"Good evening, Jude."

"G-Good evening, Master Robin." She held her trembling hands behind her back.

"Please, sit." He gestured to a wooden stool. "I'm sure you're curious as to why I asked you here, but I wanted to speak with you in private about how your lessons are progressing." Unable to reply, Jude simply nodded and let him continue. "This is a little difficult to say . . ." At those words, Jude closed her eyes and prepared herself. After all those months spent traveling to Eltham Palace, only to be asked to leave because of her inadequacy! She did not know how she could bear the shame, the disappointment. The thought flitted through her mind that at least her father was dead, and would never know.

". . . because up until now, Sir William had always insisted that I was the best musician who had come to him for training." Robin smiled warmly. "But I have to concede that honor. Your talent far surpasses my own, or at least what mine was at your age. William has asked me to inform you, Jude, that you've been chosen to perform in two different pieces at the Twelfth Night celebration this year. Our great King is expected back for the holy days, and I'm sure he'll be delighted in our latest member. What do you say to that?"

It took Jude a moment to find her voice. "Such a privilege!" she gasped finally. "I hardly know what to say!"

Robin clasped her on the shoulder. A friendly clasp, she was not too distracted to notice, not a romantic one. "Say that you'll play the lute in an instrumental quintet, and the harp while Jankin shows off his excellent soprano in a ballad. I think the harp music even has a solo piece for you, while Jankin catches his breath between verses."

" 'Tis too much." Jude was overwhelmed. She knew

from overheard conversations that the celebration of the twelfth night of Christmas was the largest festival held all year at Eltham. And if King Edward was present! There would be feasting, and plays, and mumming, but music was most important at the palace. To be chosen for not one but two pieces, and to have a solo at that, when many of the older apprentices would need to be contented with merely singing in the chorus or playing for the dances—Jude truly was astounded at her luck, as well as a little fearful of what some of the less lucky boys would say or do.

"I take all the credit, Jude, although I keep that between the two of us. You wouldn't be here if it weren't for me, aye?" At that, Robin gave her a wink and another slap on the arm. "Off to bed now. You'll need plenty of rest in the upcoming weeks."

Jude, however, was struck immobile. "You know!" she whispered.

"Of course I know! What kind of a shandy fool do you think I am, that a haircut and a tunic could disguise someone I'd met before! But don't fret, for I shan't breathe another word. Off you go now, else the others will be dying of curiosity."

On unsteady feet, Jude stumbled back to her lodgings. Someone—Matthias, she guessed—had left a candle burning, so she found her own cot without too much banging into others'.

"What did he want?" a voice whispered in the dark as she climbed into her bed, clothes and all, as she always did.

Jude couldn't identify the speaker, but she whispered back anyway, "Playing at Twelfth Night."

"Zounds! And you've been here less than a month. Aren't you lucky!"

"Aye, that I am," Jude whispered, thinking not of Twelfth Night but of Robin's hand on her shoulder.

XV

TWELFTH NIGHT

*I*f Jude thought that her relationship with Robin would be different, she was mistaken. During each lesson and rehearsal, she sought out his eyes, searching his expression for affection or   or anything to show that he viewed her as different from the other apprentices. She found nothing.

I came here for music, she told herself sternly, after another fortnight had passed and she had heard little from Robin besides "Have a seat and tune your harp, Jude, so we can get started," and the like. *And music is what I'm getting. Why do I still feel so sad?* She had achieved what she thought was her goal—but the achievement seemed flat and empty. While Jude loved her music and enjoyed her time playing more than she had ever enjoyed herself before, she had begun to feel the nagging fear that, because of her choice, she would need to give up having another kind of love in her life.

But music she did have. Rehearsals dominated the next weeks, as the minstrels and apprentices threw themselves into preparation for Twelfth Night. The other members of the palace, too, were in a panic getting ready for the King's visit, cleaning and airing the royal apartments, procuring suitable foods and wines, polishing armor and grooming horses and beating dust out of the tapestries. Jude had never seen such commotion, and she scurried through the passageways clutching her instruments protectively, for she never knew when a servant with linens piled high in her arms would crash into her, or a dozen noisy knights tramp through on their way to the tournament field.

Between regular lessons and the extra rehearsals, Jude was almost able to forget how lonely she felt. It was impossible to get to know the other apprentices, except for the little boys, like Jankin, who really didn't count in her mind. The few moments a day she could spend with Percival did little to ease her isolation. Jude wanted a friend. She thought longingly of Gwynna, and then put it out of her mind. Gilbert was too similar in appearance to her, and too different in behavior, for Jude to think much about her old friend. And unfortunately, Gilbert was also in the quintet for Twelfth Night, playing the clarion, a long type of horn Jude had never even seen before.

"Here comes the country lad," Gilbert would call out as Jude made her way into the rehearsal chamber. He would ceremonially hold out a chair for Jude, or offer to hold her instruments, or do any number of things to make Jude feel awkward and self-conscious in front of Robin and the other apprentices. If Robin weren't there, of course, Gilbert would whisk her chair away at the last second, leaving Jude in constant fear of being sent tumbling to the hard stone floor. The three other members of the quintet were friends of Gilbert's, and they, too, sneered at her when Robin's back was turned and almost made her wish she'd never been singled out for such a privilege.

Rehearsals for her other piece were leagues better. When it was just her, Jankin, Master John, and the harp, Jude could relax and throw herself into the music. She made few mistakes and earned great praise from the master—quite a difference from her quintet rehearsals, where nervousness made her clumsy and forgetful and thus even more open to Gilbert's teasing and sly pranks.

After the quintet rehearsals, Jude fell into the habit of staying late in the chamber, gathering her music slowly and going over difficult passages on the lute. That way, she could usually avoid walking out of the room with Gilbert and his friends, and perhaps even have a chance word with Robin. One evening, however, as she lingered in the chamber, she heard a foot-

217

step fall on the stone of the passageway. Jude stiffened, expecting Gilbert to return and torment her some more.

Instead, a slip of a girl poked her face into the chamber. "A good dose of hemlock in his morning cider would take care of that ragpicker," she said.

"What?"

"Gilbert. Mandrake would also work, though it's difficult to find in these parts. Dandelion would be good, too—have him in the privy all day. But hemlock would be best." She smiled at Jude and entered the room carefully. "I'm not supposed to be alone with the apprentices, but you look harmless enough. I love listening to rehearsals."

"And who might you be?" Jude asked, though the long face and dark hair gave her an inkling.

"Why, Isabel, of course. Daughter of Sir William and Lady Margaret."

"A pleasure to make your acquaintance, Lady Isabel." Jude addressed the girl respectfully, though she couldn't quite conceal her mirth at the child's combination of decorum and familiarity. "I'm Apprentice Jude."

"Lord Jude, properly," Isabel said with great seriousness. "Of Winchcombe, if I hear correctly. Skillful in harp, lute, and music composition. Less adept at Latin and mathematics. Piteous at dealing with the older apprentices."

"You hear correctly," laughed Jude. "Won't you have a seat? I assure you, I am harmless. Have you been listening in on our rehearsals for long?"

"Nay, I only returned here after St. Catherine's Day, but I'll be staying at least until the Twelfth Night festivities. Usually I live with my uncle, aunt, and cousins"—she made a face—"nearby, in Canterbury. My parents feel that Eltham isn't an appropriate place for me to grow up, what with all of you young men around, even though it's so much nicer than Uncle's drafty little manor, with all those beastly cousins underfoot. Perhaps I can convince my parents, though, to let me remain here throughout Lent. May I try your lute?"

It took Jude a moment to realize that Isabel had switched subjects. "Certainly." She handed over the lovely instrument—one of Robin's own, lent specially for the celebration.

Isabel picked a few notes, strummed part of a tune, then sighed. "They don't give girls instruments as nice as these," she explained ruefully. "We won't become professionals, of course, so we can play on any old, leftover, half-broken instrument they have lying around, even if we're as good as the apprentices."

"And you're good?" asked Jude.

"Oh, yes. How could I not be, with parents such as mine? All three of my brothers are members of the King's Minstrels, traveling and making music to their hearts' content. But my sisters are married, and I shall be too, even though I'm the youngest, and the most talented, Father says." Isabel sighed again.

Jude opened her mouth, then closed it again. Clearing her throat, she finally said, "I don't mind if you play these instruments. I think girls should have as many chances as boys do."

At that, Isabel snorted. "No wonder the other apprentices tease you." However, she clung fast to the lute. "Do you ever play duets?"

"Not here. No one wants to play with me. But it would be my honor to practice with you, Lady Isabel. If . . . if we can do it without getting into trouble."

The girl grinned at Jude. "I can manage my father, if he finds out. And as for Gilbert, and those other knaves, I really think that a dose of poison would raise you in their esteem. Put you on their level, if you know what I mean."

"I once did dose someone with hemlock and opium," Jude confided, delighted that she finally had a friend to tell her stories. "This huge blacksmith who had robbed and beaten me. But I gave him the poison only as a last resort, to save my life. I can't really justify that here."

Isabel was skeptical. "I don't know. Some of those apprentices can make life pretty difficult for a person. I've seen it all before." She gave Jude her most worldly look, then turned her attention back to the lute.

The heralds blasted their trumpet fare. Sir William boomed, "His Majesty, the King."

The King was a lot shorter than Jude had expected. He was extraordinarily handsome, however, with a trim dark beard and piercing eyes. And young; she suddenly remembered that this brilliant and severe ruler, resplendent in his ermine-trimmed robe, was barely twenty years old. However, when the King had taken his seat on the throne, high up on its dais, he looked so regal and imposing despite his youth and lack of height that Jude remembered to be frightened again.

She glanced around the now familiar great hall, hoping to catch a friendly eye to reassure her. Unfortunately, the apprentices around her were no help at all, with a trembling Jankin to her left and a stiff Gilbert to her right. Then, off to the side of the dais, Jude caught sight of a diminutive figure in green, flanked by Sir William and Lady Margaret. Isabel raised her hand as if to smooth the coils of her hair and gave Jude a discreet wave. Jude smiled back, feeling immeasurably better for having a true friend in the room. Robin, in a comely reddish brown tunic Jude hadn't seen before, was assembling the chorus for their opening song. Jude ached for him, but could not, in all honesty, count him as a friend—not when he treated her only with the same distant politeness as he did the other students.

The chorus distinguished itself, and Jude felt a swell of pride for her classmates. Then it was her turn; heart pounding, she took her seat in front of the dais, with Harold, Augustine, Jack, and of course Gilbert. Although her hands fumbled with the lute, after the opening chords of the quintet Jude was calm, losing herself to the beauty of the music. Detest Gilbert as she may, he was masterful on the clarion, and the others excelled, too, on rote, flute, and bells. All too quickly their pieces were done, and other apprentices stepped forward to take their places. Jude caught her breath, and waited expectantly by Jankin.

It was the last piece before the feasting began, the place of honor. Conscious of her duty, Jude once again bowed deeply to the King before sitting before him with her harp. Jankin, pale as she had never seen him, also bowed but remained standing. He took a long, gasping inhalation, and nodded at her to begin.

Aware of the hush in the great hall, and the hundreds of pairs of eyes on her, Jude focused with all her might on the delicate instrument in her hands. Her playing was clear and smooth, and the notes fell like raindrops onto the silent crowd. For all his nervousness, Jankin's soprano soared through the hall, moving the listeners with its range and overwhelming intensity. Thunderous applause followed their final notes, and it was with great relief that Jude put down her harp and joined Jankin to bow again to His Majesty and the other members of their audience. The two of them both were seized by tremors, and Jude gripped Jankin's hand as much to receive comfort as to give it.

"Lads," the King's voice called out over the noise of the crowds. "You do my minstrels proud. Approach." They crept up to the throne, and Jude felt Jankin's shaking increase—or perhaps it was her own. "You"— King Edward pointed at Jankin—"I have heard before. Yes?" Jankin nodded, his eyes wide and frightened. "Your skill has surpassed even last year's. 'Tis a shame a boy's voice is such a fleeting thing. But harping," here the King turned his penetrating gaze on Jude, "harping will last a lifetime. What is your name, lad?"

A gulp of air and she was able to answer, however softly. "Jude, Your Majesty. Jude of Winchcombe." It was all she could do to remember to bow again, and not curtsey.

"Welcome, young Jude, from so far away. A welcome addition to our musicians." Having done with the entertainment, King Edward turned back to the rest of his subjects. "And now let the feasting begin!"

It was the longest night Jude could ever remember, between the feasting and wassailing, toasting and mumming. His Majesty roared with laughter when aged Master Alfred and one of the youngest serving girls found the special beans in their Twelfth Night cakes and thus were chosen as King and Queen of the

Bean. The blushing pair was paraded around the hall before being seated together at the dais and served next to King Edward himself. By the time the actors had mummed the play of the three Wise Men, Jude's head was spinning from relief and disappointment that her part was over, as well as from the unaccustomed amount of wine she had drunk at the feast. In the corner of her consciousness, too, was the mounting hostility of some of the older apprentices, mainly Gilbert and his friends. Perhaps her suspicions were brought on by a wine-befuddled brain, but Jude was convinced that the other students were whispering about her, and none too favorably, she guessed, by the looks they shot her way. Were they jealous of the King's praise? she wondered. Or was it more? Jude felt only great relief when Sir William finally announced the festivities over; she avoided the knots of students who lingered to sing some more, and instead went to her cot more bone-weary than she'd been since her first day at Eltham.

"Jude. Jude! Wake up—you'll be late for first Mass!"

Someone was shaking her, jarring her sore head, causing jabs of pain to prick behind her eyelids. With one swift movement she sat up, grabbed the earthen jug she kept next to her bed, and vomited profusely into it. Still retching, she heard the other apprentices' laughter, and her face burned with both shame and her discomfort. Why had she drunk so much wine last night? Drained, Jude lay back on her cot and groaned softly.

Jankin, however, was not to be put off. "Sir William will be angry if you miss morning prayers," he continued, but got no reaction besides Jude's covering her face with her hands to block out the dawn's light. He disappeared then, only to return moments later with a dented pewter cup. "Drink," he ordered, and Jude gladly gulped down the cider, hoping it would stay down. With a touching gentleness, Jankin got her up, straightened her clothes and hair, and helped her wash her hands and face. Then, prodding Jude down the passageway, he led her toward the chapel.

"I needed to talk to you," he whispered, fumbling with his belt pouch. "Master Robin gave me this. He couldn't find you after the festival last night, and said he hadn't time to visit the apprentices' lodgings. He said it was important I gave this to you in private, before the day began." Puffed up with the weight and secrecy of his task, Jankin produced a small set of pipes.

Jude's skin crawled as she wordlessly took the pipes and hid them under her tunic. The hard wood poked her throughout Mass. She said her prayers mechanically and had to be prodded by Jankin to get up from her pew and take communion. As the members of the palace filed out of the chapel and toward the great hall for breakfast, Jude freed herself from the group and slipped away, into an empty cloister. There, in the cold of a January morning, she held the set of pipes up to the light. She knew what to look for this time.

The parchment was in the same place—folded tightly into the smallest reed. Again it was in French, but the message was a much less welcome one than Robin's of last spring, which had beckoned her to Eltham. She read:

I am called away on family business and do not know when I shall return. Be mindful while I am gone. There are those who wish to harm you. R

Once more Robin had drawn the outline of a lute after his initial. Jude stared at the small missive and had to lean against the cold stone wall to control her trembling. The warning that she was in danger barely penetrated her thoughts. All she could focus on was that Robin was gone.

XVI

ROBIN

"*M*aster Robin has been called away due to personal concerns," Sir William announced in the great hall at the end of breakfast. Jude had slipped in just as the assembled apprentices were finishing; no matter, for she couldn't have stomached cold mutton that morning anyway. Sir William looked as sour as Jude felt, and she wondered if Robin had left any more explanation with the Master than with her. "Apprentice Geoffrey will be instructing Master Robin's students in the meantime, since the other instrument masters are journeying as minstrels." A solemn youth, ready to begin his first rounds of travel in the spring, Geoffrey nodded at the older students who would now be in his charge. With a sigh Jude rose and followed him to one of the small practice chambers.

Robin gone, Twelfth Night over, dour Geoffrey as her new master—Jude felt no enthusiasm for returning to her music. Between heartsickness and the effects of her drinking last night, she wished fervently to return to bed for a week, at least.

The days seemed so long. Geoffrey either didn't notice how much Gilbert harassed Jude, or he simply turned a blind eye to it, unwilling or unable to interfere. Instrumental lessons, once such a joy, were bitter hours to be endured. With rehearsals for Twelfth Night finished, and none scheduled yet for the St. Valentine's Day festival, Jude thought she might have extra time to spend composing, or at least hunting with Percival. Unfortunately, Master Hal had different ideas; he set upon her one day with a thick, darkened volume, its pages ratty and coming loose from the binding.

"My Cicero," he explained reverently. "Passed down from my father to me. Copied by another relative, now long gone, but undoubtedly one in Holy Orders. This Cicero has seen much use, lad, over the years, but now I'm afraid it is turning to dust, as we all must in time." Hal stopped to stare forlornly at the volume. "So," he continued abruptly, "your hand is acceptable, and as you will never make a scholar, I am turning over to you the task of recopying this manuscript. Two or three hours a day should be sufficient. You ought to be finished within a year or so."

"But . . . ," Jude began helplessly.

Master Hal waved away her objections. "I have taken the liberty of securing enough parchment and ink for the copying. Do not make mistakes, for the materials are very dear. My brother, the monk, will be pleased to bind the pages when you are done. Perhaps this will instill in you some respect for the great Roman philosophers."

Wordlessly she took the decrepit volume.

O praeclarum custodem ovium lupum! Jude copied diligently by candlelight in the cold, empty chamber. She had learned during the past anxious, tedious weeks not to sigh out loud, for her breath would make the candle flicker and drip, thus spattering wax on her precious sheets of Cicero.

A shadow fell across her page. " 'An excellent protector of sheep, the wolf,' " translated Gilbert. "How appropriate. Master Hal has sent me to fetch you—he insists that you are late with his latest manuscript pages." Smirking, he made a grab for the top pieces of parchment.

Jude wasn't fast enough, and before she knew it, Gilbert had retreated to a corner of the room with her work. "Hmm," he said, "this one's not quite dry yet." He dragged his hand across the page, then, smiling, held up ink-smeared fingertips.

"Give me those!" She made a desperate leap for the

pages, but Gilbert held them high in the air and pushed her away with his other hand. As Jude stumbled into the chair and tried to regain her balance, she saw Gilbert bring his hands together to crush the sheets.

"No!" In horror and fury, Jude launched herself again at the other apprentice, this time intent more on hurting him than on retrieving her work. She hadn't counted on Gilbert's knife.

Tossing the mangled parchment aside, he whipped a six-inch steel blade out of his boot top. Jude retreated, reaching for her own belt knife, but finding the pouch empty. By Mary, where was her knife? Not that her small blade, used only for cutting meat at mealtimes, would do much good against that dagger Gilbert was brandishing, but she still cursed her carelessness.

Jude ducked and threw herself at Gilbert's legs when he lunged at her, and they both went tumbling to the ground. Although Jude was tall, she was no match in height or weight for the older apprentice. Within seconds, he had the blade held across her throat, pinning her to the stone floor.

Once again Jude cursed the palace rules that did not allow her to keep Percival by her side at all times. The falcon would have reduced Gilbert's skin to bloody shreds. As she was alone, however, she ceased to struggle lest her opponent press the knife farther into her neck.

"What makes you think you can take me on? That you can simply appear out of nowhere and suddenly be a favorite of the masters and the King? Well, things will be different here from now on, with Robin gone. No one is looking after you now, Jude of Winchcombe." He spat out the name. "I don't know who you really are, but you'd better watch yourself. Do you understand?"

Jude nodded her comprehension, not trusting herself to speak, then stood slowly when Gilbert released her. Grabbing the remaining parchment from the table, Jude sped out of the room. But her last glance at Gilbert filled her with an even deeper dread. The expression on his face—a confused, wondering look—made her fear the worst.

And in fact, realization was slowly dawning on Gilbert, though he dared not believe his senses. In their brief wrestle, he had felt in Jude a difference, a softness . . . Jude did not seem to be built quite like the other lads. Gilbert shook his head sharply, telling himself he simply imagined it. Yet somehow, he could not fully shake off his suspicions.

I must get out of here, Jude thought desperately. But how? How could she travel in the middle of winter? And how could she disappear, not knowing where Robin was?

The next weeks were agony for Jude. With Gilbert's

threats echoing in her ears, she refused a lute solo that Apprentice Geoffrey offered her for the St. Valentine's Day festival, accepting instead a small harp part to accompany the chorus. She felt infinitely safer in a large group, working with other musicians. Rehearsing with Geoffrey did not have the same appeal as practicing with Robin—or even Sir William; and anyway Jude was constantly being berated by Master Hal for her sluggishness as a scribe. As hard as she worked on her Cicero, she could never keep up to his demands, not the least because her parchment sheets disappeared on a regular basis, and her quills were broken, and ink spilled or ruined by being mixed with ale.

"It's not just Gilbert," Isabel reported late one afternoon as she slipped carefully into the mews, where Jude was working, sitting on a stool with her copy materials laid out precariously in front of her. It was quite cold, and the light was terrible to work by, but simply having Percival on her shoulder was an unbelievable comfort. "It sounds as though Jack and Augustine are in on these beastly pranks, too."

"I suspected as much," replied Jude with a sigh, trying to wipe some of the ink from her fingers with a filthy scrap of cloth. "How did you find out?"

"No one notices a girl," she said scornfully. "But even my father and the other masters can see that something is wrong with you. Father is quite worried, in fact, though with Robin absent he hasn't had time to do anything about it. Why won't you say something to him?"

Jude simply shook her head. Men, she thought bitterly, were supposed to fight their own battles, so that was what she must do.

Jankin was also concerned about Jude, though he was careful not to show it, lest he, too, become a scapegoat. He had hoped that once Jude was no longer "the new apprentice," Gilbert and his friends would cease to bother Jude, but that was not the case. Late January brought two more lads to Eltham—brothers from Bath, the youngest sons of a well-to-do merchant. Hugh, the elder, had already at sixteen a vibrant baritone, while Maurice, two years his junior, was adept at the flute and other wind instruments. As their oldest two brothers were taking over the family business, and their middle brother was a novitiate in the Church, Hugh and Maurice were packed off by their father for musical training and—more significantly—to consort with people of breeding. Unfortunately for Jude (and for Hugh and Maurice's father, who had hopes that the rascals would learn some manners), the newest apprentices fell right in with Gilbert's crowd.

The tricks played on Jude increased, and the threats became more direct. Jude rolled up her bedding and her extra clothes, and took to spending her nights on the icy floor of the mews. With Percival beside her, and the other falcons and hawks in their cages lining the walls, she was able to sleep more soundly than in a warm cot in the apprentices' lodgings.

Jude's disappointment was no less bitter just because she had known grief before. Her father's death, her mother's quick remarriage, being sent off to school, her forced betrothal: all had caused her sorrow and anguish. But of Eltham she had expected great things, had planned to make her life and home there. It was unthinkable now, but she had no other plans, no other dreams that seemed attainable. Her saint's day had come and gone in the autumn, and she was now fourteen. Of marriageable age, but with no prospects of even a place to live.

"Maybe I should pray to St. Jude," she said aloud to Percival one lonely night. "Patron saint of the hopeless. Perhaps he'd help more than Mary and her Son."

Prayers, however, brought no lessening of the harassment she received at the hands of the other apprentices; if anything, the assaults increased as winter progressed. When she discovered one morning that all the strings on her harp had been cut, she made her decision: she would be on the road again when the weather broke, Robin or no Robin. However much she might want to go right then, traveling in February without a horse, without shelter, and without money to

pay for lodgings would be both foolhardy and dangerous. A few more weeks and the frost should lift. A few
more weeks, and perhaps Robin would return, and she
could at least say a proper good-bye.

Diligently she repaired her harp and attended rehearsals, guarded her copyists' supplies and transcribed
Cicero, watched her fellow apprentices and prepared
herself for more travel, this time to an unknown desti-
nation. St. Valentine's Day approached, and although
the King and his brother were both away, Eltham was
again hosting a courtly celebration. Lady Margaret and
her servants were occupied decorating the great hall
with scented candles and carved lanterns, with the
kitchen staff hurrying to cook leeks, figs, pomegran-
ates, and other dishes to tempt lovers. These specialties,
of course, were reserved for the masters and their honored guests, since the "foods of Venus" were considered inappropriate for the youthful and unmarried
apprentices. Spiced ale and other festival foods would
be served, however, so even the young could partake in
the feast, and the whole company would be invited to
play St. Valentine's Day games.

Because she was one of the musicians performing at
the festival, Jude dutifully pinned a lover's knot on her
tunic, to match the other apprentices. The pair of fabric circles mocked her own gloomy state, and she was
glad to take her well-hidden seat next to the rote

player and wait for the chorus, up on their high platform, to begin. At least the music would distract her, and the singers would perform all afternoon.

The musicians played excellently and rested only during the vocal solos. Master John had arranged a hauntingly lovely duet called *"Amor Vincit Omnia"* ("Love Conquers All") for soprano and tenor; Jude was so swept up in the music she didn't hear a footfall behind her until it was too late. A hand clapped over her mouth prevented her from crying out, and other rough hands pulled her from her chair and dragged her underneath the dais. Jankin's high treble came to her muffled through the fabric draped around the platform; her friend was singing, and no one else would help her. In the dim interior under the dais, Jude's eyes adjusted and she faced her adversaries with outward calm and internal dread.

"What now, Gilbert? What have I done to offend you today?" she whispered. "I have but a small part in the festivities: neither master nor King shall see my face."

"Neither master nor King shall ever see your face again if you don't speak to me with more respect, you young ragpicker!" breathed Gilbert.

Jack grabbed Jude's arms and pinned them behind her back. Afraid that loud noises would distract the singers and call attention to her embarrassing predicament, Jude held her tongue while the brawny lad clutched her harshly. She noticed Hugh, the newest apprentice, and Augustine crouching next to Gilbert, the crowded dais unable to accommodate them comfortably.

Gilbert unsheathed his knife—the one with which Jude was already so familiar—and brandished it under her nose. "Tell us who you really are, young Jude. So young, aren't you? Eleven years, according to Sir William. That would explain your lack of beard, your high voice. Tell us the truth, you imp, or we shall be forced to reveal you ourselves!" He dragged the tip of his knife down the front of Jude's tunic, and Jude caught her breath, expecting any moment to hear the tearing of fabric.

Instead she heard a faint voice through the draperies around the dais, and then saw the material part and a shaft of light stream in. "Jude, what are you doing?" Matthias demanded, squinting at the scene in front of him. "You'll miss your next entrance. Jack's already skipped two of his passages; Sir William will be hopping mad when he finds you were fooling around instead of minding your instruments!"

Reluctantly Jack released his grip on Jude's arms, and she slipped away with Matthias as the others returned to their positions. "You saved my skin," she whispered gratefully to the young apprentice, before taking up her seat again.

He shrugged and held up his flute. "My part sounds

terrible without the harp accompaniment." With a smile and a wink, he too returned to his chair.

Several songs passed before Jude had control of her breathing again. *I must go immediately after the feasting—just slip out to the mews, take Percival, and be on my way. Perhaps I can find a barn for shelter,* she thought, shivering at the idea of sleeping outside in the February damp and cold. It would be risky to go, but clearly, more dangerous to stay. She would fortify herself at the feast and then say farewell to Eltham.

When the time came for the musicians to leave their hidden posts and take seats around the feasting tables of the great hall, Jude was flanked by Matthias and Jankin. *My tiny protectors,* she thought with wry amusement. *Perhaps there is safety in company.* Forcing herself to eat—not knowing when her next meal would be—Jude barely noticed the jugglers and other performers who circled the hall to amuse the feasters.

The heart-shaped cakes were being served when there was suddenly a great commotion at the south entrance. Jude looked up from the crumb-strewn table to behold a mass of people crowding the door. Sir William uttered a joyful shout and went plowing through the throng. Jude and her tablemates were on their feet, craning to see.

"What is it?" Matthias asked.

Jankin, climbing up on the bench for a better view, answered. "By my Lady, it's Robin!"

Her heart beating wildly, Jude sat down heavily on the bench, nearly knocking Jankin off.

"Lords, ladies, and apprentices!" Sir William called. "Our banquet is now made even more blessed, by the presence of our dear Master Robin." Enthusiastic applause greeted the introduction, and Robin, looking weary and travel-stained, mounted the dais to address the crowd.

"My dear friends," he began, "I am honored by this welcome, but distressed to interrupt your feasting with sad news. I have come not to resume my work as one of the King's Minstrels, but instead to say farewell." Robin held up his hands to quiet the murmuring of the crowd.

"My elder brother has been taken by the fever. I was summoned by his wife, many weeks ago, to be at his side as he lay dying. As a younger son I had been allowed to follow my dream and pursue a life of music; however, the obligation to my family must come first, for now that my brother is gone there is no other male to rule our estates until my young nephew comes of age. My brother's wife has begged that I return to Suffolk immediately to take charge of our family's lands. I cannot refuse my duty." Gravely he turned to Sir William. "Tonight, I must relinquish my position as a master of the King's Minstrels. I shall never forget you, or any of the others who have made my life here so happy. But I must pack my belongings and leave in the morning, to serve the King as a feudal lord instead of a musician." He bowed deeply and stepped off the dais.

A stunned silence in the audience was followed by a rousing shout, led by Sir William. "Three cheers for Robin!"

"Hurrah! Hurrah! Hurrah!" the crowd responded.

"Long live the King!" called Sir William.

"Long live the King!" The assembled masters and apprentices all crowded around Robin to wish him luck and Godspeed. In the commotion, Jude slipped away, unnoticed.

"I've been waiting for you to come."

Jude held her finger to her lips and closed the heavy door to Robin's chamber. She slid her pack to the floor and moved Percival from her arm to perch instead on a chair. "I was avoiding some of the other apprentices. You were right to warn me. The mews have been a safer place for me these weeks than the lodgings."

Robin nodded and continued to pack his belongings. In the candlelight, he looked tired and somber, much older than his years. The two stood in awkward silence.

"I didn't know your family held feudal estates," Jude began.

"You're not the only nobility here, Lady Judith," replied Robin tartly.

Chastened, Jude did not reply. She simply watched him, her thoughts in a turmoil. This was not how she had pictured their meeting, or their farewell. Remembering why she was there, however, she finally found her voice again. "I . . . I wanted to wish you safe travels, Master Robin. And to thank you for your note. Your notes."

Abruptly Robin looked up from his sack. "Have you been in much danger?"

"Gilbert and his friends, including the two newest apprentices. Their threats are becoming less veiled—I believe that they know my secret." She sighed and ran her hand along Percival's feathers to calm herself. "So I must leave, before morning. I'd hate to think what would happen to me if I were revealed as a female before Sir William and the other masters."

"Where will you go?" Robin's voice was steady, almost casual, as he asked.

Jude shrugged. "To London." She remembered uneasily that Lady Christina was in London. "Or perhaps Canterbury. I had made no plans for life after Eltham. I simply must go."

"And what will you do in London or Canterbury?" He looked Jude up and down with a critical eye. "You won't be able to pass as a boy for much longer."

Blushing, Jude turned to hide her face. "As I said, I have no plans yet. Perchance I can find work as a tavern maid. Or possibly someone will want my skills in Latin and math." The bitterness in her voice almost made Robin flinch.

"You are a gifted musician," he reminded her softly, "and an extraordinary composer. Do not despair that you'll have to give up your music, any more than I should grieve that I must give up mine. There are other ways than being one of the King's Minstrels."

Remembering that Robin, too, was leaving his life's work, and that he was still in mourning for his brother, Jude felt ashamed. "Forgive me my self-indulgence. I was thinking only of myself."

With a nod, Robin acknowledged her apology. "Your position is a difficult one, young Jude. For, although it is not in the place of my choosing, I at least will have a roof over my head and food in my belly. But you . . . how many nobles would want a female minstrel?"

"How many, indeed?" Jude responded. Despondent, she moved to pick up her pack.

Gently Robin answered his own question. "I, for one."

Jude looked up abruptly. "What?"

"I want a female minstrel. Not just any female minstrel—I want you, Jude. Will you come with me to my family's manor?"

Her heart pounding, Jude could barely stammer out her response. "Y-Yes! Yes, of course!" Tears of gratitude came to her eyes. She wouldn't starve, or be

242

forced to earn her living in degrading ways. And most important, she would see Robin every day, play for him at the manor, talk with him in the evenings . . . "Nothing would delight me more than being your minstrel."

"Oh, but it isn't simply as a musician that I want you, Jude. I hope that you will also be my wife."

Jude grabbed at the chair back to steady herself. Percival let out an annoyed squawk as his perch was upset by Jude's fumbling. "What?" she said again, even more stunned this time.

Robin moved to her side and held out his hands for her to take. "Will you be my wife, Lady Judith? I know you bring no money and no family connections. But your music is enough of a dowry for me. We can publish the banns when we reach Suffolk and be married in the spring. What is your answer, dear Jude?"

"Why? Why would you want to marry me?"

"Because I love you. I've loved you since I first saw you, at that awful betrothal banquet. I could hardly contain myself and not slay that disgusting old man you were supposed to wed. But I was the King's emissary . . . and all I could do was give you a chance, let you know that there was another place to go."

"Did you really think I would come? Did you believe I could make such a long and difficult journey?"

Robin shook his head. "No, but I hoped. And I was right. Am I right now, Judith, in thinking that perhaps

243

you could love me and be my wife?" Without waiting for a response, he leaned forward and gave her a gentle kiss.

Flustered, Jude turned her head away and tried to free her hands from his. She had never been kissed before. "Could you stand having such a willful wife? A wife who knew she could make her own way in the world? I am not the dutiful young woman you met almost a year ago."

"Aye, but even then you were a rebellious child—I remember clearly how you called both your stepfather and your betrothed louts. Not the behavior of an obedient daughter. And I fell in love with you anyway." He asked again, "Will you marry me?"

"Robin, I vowed to myself that nothing would make me give up music. This is how I can best serve God. Perhaps it is not my lot in life to be a wife and mother. What man would want to be wed to a minstrel?"

"I would, Jude. How many ways can I say it? Why would I want a wife who didn't understand my own passion for music, my need to compose and play?"

"But the lord of the manor needs a lady who can run the household, not just tune on a harp. I have no interest in seeing to servants and banquets, in . . . in checking the quality of the butter and keeping the herb pantry stocked."

"My sister-in-law will still be the mistress of our manor, if that's what we wish. I swear to you, by

Mary's veil, that you will have all the time you need for music. Do you love me, Jude? If you do, say that you'll share your life with me."

Unable to look at him, Jude leaned her forehead against his chest. "I love you, Robin. I, too, fell in love at that betrothal banquet. But I couldn't bring myself to admit it, for I seemed to have no choice. Either a life as a musician or one as a wife—I didn't know I could have them both." Heart pounding, Jude forced herself to meet Robin's eyes. "Yes, I will marry you."

They kissed again, but this time Jude didn't pull away. When they parted she looked out the slit of a window and noticed the position of the moon. "It's almost dawn, and I must go. Where shall we meet?"

Robin peered at the sky for a moment before answering. "The small bridge is the least guarded, so try your luck leaving that way, through the kitchens. The servants should be up at this hour."

Picturing the kitchen bridge in her mind, Jude said, "That will put me on the west side of Eltham. Where should I go from there?"

"Circle around through the woods until you reach the northern path. I'll say my final farewells before Mass and meet you with two horses. From there, we can easily reach the Dover Road."

"Hurry," Jude told him as she fastened on her pack. "Come before they notice I'm gone."

Robin ran his hand through Jude's blond curls,

brushing them off her forehead. "Perhaps I should explain to Sir William . . ."

"And tell him what? That you knew I was female all along? That we intentionally deceived him? No. I'll send a note of explanation when we're safely away from here. I've done that before." She sighed, thinking too of Isabel, Matthias, and Jankin—the young friends who had helped her so much those past months—and wishing she could say a proper farewell. Then a wry smile twitched at the corners of her mouth, as she pictured Gilbert's chagrin when he discovered she was gone. *Poor Gilbert,* she thought. *He'll have no one left to torment.*

"All right." Robin was nodding his agreement to her plan. "But be careful in the woods alone."

Jude laughed softly and brushed her lips against his, murmuring, "I've been in the woods alone more days and nights than I can count. I'll be fine, my love. Just impatient for you to join me."

"Aye, that I understand. Make haste now, darling Jude. I will not tarry here without you."

They kissed a final time; then Jude placed Percival back on her shoulder and crept into the hall. Her heart pounded as she made her way out of the palace and slipped stealthily into the woods. She barely breathed again until the sun was up and she heard hooves on the earth and saw Robin appear on his gray horse, leading

246

a dappled brown for her. She mounted the horse with a leap, unable to speak for the lump in her throat. The two minstrels smiled at each other, then guided their horses to the north, each assured that a life filled with music and love lay before them.

ABOUT THE AUTHOR

BERIT HAAHR is a writer and teacher who lives in Pennsylvania. She hopes someday to learn to play the harp.